THEY CLASHED AT FORT VERDE

Mark Shields—Haunted by the heroic reputation of a long-dead father, he had to choose between duty and disgrace, between his Eastern fiancée and the most beautiful woman in Arizona—a white Apache.

Sasha Quiet Stream—Saved as a young girl by an Apache chief, this white child was raised in the ancient traditions of her stepfather's tribe. Then she fell in love with Mark Shields, who was compelled by duty to destroy her people.

Manitoro—The most brutal Apache warrior in Arizona Territory, he killed to obliterate his astounding past.

Chatoma—The bold Indian who tried to be at peace with his fearful white neighbors, even though most of them would rather see him dead.

Farley Branson—As a practical businessman, he balanced profit and loss. His profit in land would mean the loss of hundreds of lives. That sounded just fine.

The Stagecoach Series
Ask your bookseller for the books you have missed

STAGECOACH STATION 39:

FORT VERDE

Hank Mitchum

™ Created by the producers of
**Wagons West, White Indian,
Badge,** and **Winning the West.**

Book Creations Inc., Canaan, NY · Lyle Kenyon Engel, Founder

BANTAM BOOKS
TORONTO · NEW YORK · LONDON · SYDNEY · AUCKLAND

STAGECOACH STATION 39: FORT VERDE

*A Bantam Book / published by arrangement with
Book Creations, Inc.*

Bantam edition / January 1989

Produced by Book Creations, Inc.
Lyle Kenyon Engel: Founder

ISBN 0-553-27643-3

Published simultaneously in the United States and Canada

PRINTED IN THE UNITED STATES OF AMERICA

O   0 9 8 7 6 5 4 3 2 1

STAGECOACH STATION 39:
FORT VERDE

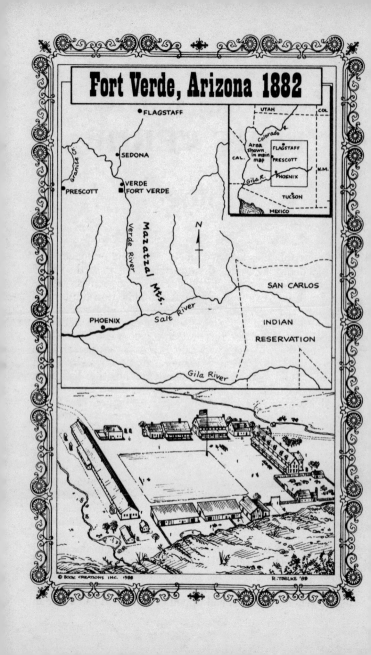

Fort Verde, Arizona 1882

Prologue

The terrible noises had stopped. She could no longer hear the bloodcurdling yells, the terrifying screams, the sharp crack of gunfire, the whistle and thud of arrows, or the thunder of hooves that had kept her huddled on the ground with her arms over her head. Now the only sound that reached her ears was the whimpering moan of the wind as it whirled around the overturned Conestoga wagon hiding her.

Trembling, five-year-old Lily Mason pulled herself from between the shattered boards of the unburned wagon, and then peered around at the ruins of the six wagons that had been their wagon train. She felt tears running down her cheeks, and she swallowed a sob, trying to be very quiet. Her father had made her promise to do that—to be very, very quiet—when he saw the bad men with painted faces riding across the desert to attack them.

Lying a few yards away among some tattered canvas was the fluttering calico of her mother's dress. Lily wiped her blue eyes with her sleeve and crawled over to her. She leaned against a broken wheel and picked up her mother's hand. Squeezing the fingers as hard as she could, she wondered why her mother did not squeeze back, or talk to her, or move.

All around her mother, arrows were stuck in the ground and in the broken wagons. Her father lay nearby with several arrows protruding from his back. When she called to him, begging him to come to her, he did not answer, nor did he move. When the wagon had tipped over, he had had a rifle in his hands, but his hands were empty now, as were the hands of the men from the other wagons.

There were no arrows in her mother but there was blood on the side of her head. Lily could see some of the women from the other wagons, and like her mother they were quiet and still. There had been children on the wagons, too, but all of them were like the adults, lying quiet and still.

Suddenly she remembered her brother. She did not see him anywhere and wondered if she should look for him, but just now she was too frightened to let go of her mother's hand.

It had been May of 1866 when she and her family left St. Joseph, Missouri. Lily and her mother, father, and six-year-old brother, Jimmy, had joined a wagon train bound for California. When they started out, Lily had not known where California was, or even what California was, but she had often heard her parents making plans for the house they would have and the beautiful garden they would grow when they got there. She was very excited, and every morning she would ask her mother and father if they would get to California that day.

Not every wagon was going to California. At various places along the route, groups of wagons left the wagon train, their owners either deciding to stay where they were or heading out on their own for other destinations. Lily felt sorry for the people who left, because they would not have the fine house, the wonderful garden, and the beautiful flowers she was going to have. There had been dozens of wagons when they started, but now the last six had been attacked by Indians in a place her father called Arizona Territory.

Lily did not fully understand death, but she knew something awful had happened. And she knew that of all the people who had been on the wagons—her mother, father, Jimmy, Mr. and Mrs. Clark, her friend and playmate Sally, Mr. Petrey, the wagon boss, and all the others—only she remained. She was alone now, and she was frightened.

Over the sound of the moaning wind Lily heard the pounding of approaching hoofbeats. When she looked up and saw the riders, she thought it was the bad men returning to hurt and burn again. She curled up against her mother, closed her eyes, and pretended to be asleep. Maybe if they believed she was being a good girl and taking her nap, they would leave her alone.

She kept her eyes closed very tightly for a very long time. When she opened them, she saw a man squatting in front of her. His clothing and features were like those of the bad men, but his eyes were kind. Lily could not understand evil or prejudice or the enmity that existed between Indians and whites, but she could understand kind. When the kind Indian spoke softly and reached out his arms to her, she smiled and raised her arms to be enfolded. She was glad, at last, to have someone who would hold and comfort her.

One of the Indians said something, but he spoke such strange words that Lily could not understand what he was saying. Then she saw that he was pointing to her mother's hand. The Indian who was holding Lily said something in reply, and Lily watched as they slipped her mother's gold ring from her finger and then cut a long lock of her mother's golden hair. The hair was deftly braided into a tiny rope, which was looped through the ring and tied around Lily's neck.

As the Indians took her away from the place of destruction, Lily looked back. She knew she would never see her mother, father, brother, or friends again. She was very sad, but she tried to hold back the tears. When the bad Indians had come, her father had told her to be brave. She was being as brave as she could be.

Chapter One

In the painted desert of northern Arizona, a lone Indian on horseback watched the approaching train. It was traveling at the respectable speed of fifty miles an hour, but against the vast terrain, the train appeared merely to be crawling—a tiny silhouette with smoke that poured from its stack drawing a thin pencil line across the bright blue vault of sky.

After a few moments the Indian could hear the train quite clearly, the chugging of its engine reaching him across the wide, flat plain. Then, as it approached, it gave proof to the vastness of the land, for the train that had been so tiny before was now a behemoth, blocking out the sky.

Seeing the Indian, the engineer blew his whistle in greeting, and the great train rushed past at tremendous speed, smoke and steam trailing behind in long wisps, its huge driver wheels pounding along the rails. The blast of air and noise from its passing hit the Indian with the impact of a sudden desert sandstorm, and he turned his back to the train until the last car flashed by.

"Oh, did you see him?" a well-dressed woman in the parlor car called excitedly. "It was an Indian!"

"That's what you ought to draw," the woman's husband, a rather large man with a walrus-style mustache, said to the young army lieutenant sitting across from the couple. The tall, dark-haired young man had been sketching with practiced ease throughout the journey from Chicago. With his feet perched on the seat opposite him, he created an easel with his bent legs and rested his sketch pad against them.

5

"Who are you to tell him what to draw?" the woman asked her husband. "I think the Chicago train shed he is drawing is quite lovely."

"That's Chicago?"

"Of course it is. Don't you recognize it?"

In the picture, the lieutenant had recreated the interior of the train shed with its beehive of activity. He had skillfully captured the people in the scene with only smudges and strokes of charcoal, but each stroke, whether to depict a person or the network of cables overhead or the skylights above them, made the picture come alive with a startling reality.

In the lower right-hand corner of the picture, he had lettered "Chicago Train Shed, Summer 1882." Beneath that he had signed his name, Mark Shields.

"Mrs. Solinger, this is for you," Shields said, handing the drawing to the woman with a smile.

"For me? Whatever for?" the attractive, middle-aged woman asked, blushing at the attention shown her by the handsome, much-younger army officer.

"Why, for being so kind as to invite me to be your whist partner," Shields explained. She and her husband, a banker, were returning to California from a visit to New York and had been congenial traveling companions throughout the long journey.

"You are being too generous," her husband said with a laugh. "She caused you to lose the game."

"Yes, but never was defeat suffered in such gracious company," Shields replied, gallantly bowing his head.

"The conductor said we would be arriving in Prescott in a little over an hour," Mrs. Solinger said. "You'll be getting off there?"

"Yes," Shields answered. "I'm being posted to duty at Fort Verde."

"Well," Mrs. Solinger said, "I know you are a soldier, but I can't help but feel you could have a wonderful career as an artist. You have entertained the entire train with your marvelous talent. Don't you think he should be an artist, Sam?" she asked her husband.

"Dear, don't fill his head with your foolish prattle," Solinger replied. "I can understand a man's being called to arms. I sometimes regret that I have never heard the bugle's call myself. The life of a soldier on the frontier can be very exciting for a young man. Am I right, Lieutenant?"

Shields's smile was self-deprecating. "I wouldn't know, sir," he admitted. "I only recently graduated from West Point. This will be my first assignment."

"Well, then, think of the adventure that awaits you," Solinger suggested. "And you are a graduate of the military academy. How proud your father must be of you."

"I'm sure he would be, sir, but my father is deceased."

"Oh, I'm sorry. Please excuse me," Mr. Solinger, flustered, said hurriedly.

Shields's smile put Solinger at ease. "I hardly remember my father," he explained. "He was killed nineteen years ago at Gettysburg."

"At Gettysburg? And your name is Shields? See here, are you by any chance related to Colonel Benjamin Shields?"

"Benjamin Shields was my father."

"Lieutenant, let me shake your hand," Solinger said with enthusiasm. "Martha, did you have any idea we were riding with such a celebrity? Why, it is said that President Lincoln himself, when he gave his Gettysburg address, asked to visit Colonel Shields's grave site. Mr. G. W. Finely in his *Commentaries on Gettysburg* credits Colonel Shields with the pivotal act that guaranteed victory for the Union. I must confess, I'm somewhat of a military student," Solinger explained to him.

"Your knowledge of military history is impressive, and I do appreciate your kind words about my father," Shields replied self-consciously. "But the heroism was his, not mine. You needn't feel honored by my presence."

Shields thought again of how his life had been shaped by the heroic deeds of a man who was little more to him than a photograph on the mantel or a chapter in a history book. But the image of his father had always haunted him: During his course on tactics at West Point, an entire unit had been devoted to a detailed examination of his father's Gettysburg maneuvers.

A man that Shields could barely remember had been held up to him as a model for his entire life. Everything he did was measured against the standard his father had set. Shields was proud of his father, but he resented the constant comparison. Even his career as an army officer was more or less chosen for him. Mrs. Solinger had no idea how close to the truth she had come when she suggested that he should be an artist rather than a soldier.

Shields had honed his artistic skill as a magazine free-lancer during his years at West Point. An admirer of Winslow Homer, he had sent some of his work to the artist, who had forwarded Shields's drawings to *Harper's Weekly*, where Homer had been an artist-correspondent during the war. Ironically, even there Shields's father's name had served him well, for Winslow Homer had once spent a month in the field with the elder Shields and felt a debt of gratitude, which he repaid by recommending Shields to his former employer.

"Mr. and Mrs. Solinger, your table is ready," a porter said, coming into the car.

"Oh, won't you join us for this last meal?" Mrs. Solinger asked the lieutenant.

"No, thank you," Shields said, shaking his head and smiling. "I think I'll skip lunch. I have a few things to do before I get off the train."

"Very well, Lieutenant," Mr. Solinger said, as he stood up to move to the dining car. "If you get off before we return, I do wish you good luck in your career."

"Thank you."

Shields did not really have anything to do; he merely wanted a few minutes to be alone and gather his thoughts. The trip west had been hot and tiring, and he was pleased that it was almost at an end. He would be equally glad when his tour of duty at Fort Verde was completed so he could return to Washington to serve on Brigadier General Schuyler Hamilton's staff. General Hamilton was the father of Shields's fiancée, Susan.

At the thought of Susan, Shields reached into his pocket and took out his watch. He opened the case and gazed at the small photograph of Susan that was tucked inside the cover. Even in the photograph she was a very pretty young woman, and as he looked at her he thought ahead to the next few weeks. Susan would be arriving at Fort Verde as soon as he could make arrangements for their wedding and obtain suitable lodgings for them at the fort.

"Though wives are not authorized by regulations at remote posts in the West, their presence is sanctioned by unofficial understanding," Shields's *Officers' Guide* read.

"Young officers must always be aware, however, of the custom of 'ranking out,' meaning that to the higher ranking officer go the better accommodations. A newly commissioned second lieutenant might be well advised to wait a prudent period of time before undertaking the responsibility of a wife."

"As far as I'm concerned, two weeks *is* a prudent period of time," Susan had told him firmly when he showed her the passage. "After all, I am a general's daughter, and that should count for something."

"When you marry me, you will no longer be a general's daughter. You'll be a second lieutenant's wife," Shields had reminded her gently.

"Nonsense. I shall always be who I am," she had replied, closing the discussion.

Shields had been unsettled by this journey west. Though he was accustomed to the comforts of the East and was not looking foward to the assignment, he had been captivated by the strange beauty of the land and its inhabitants. During the solitude of the journey he had drawn a series of detailed sketches of western life. Although he had given the sketch of the Chicago train shed to Mrs. Solinger, he had many other completed drawings tucked away in his portfolio. He was thinking about submitting them to some of the magazines that had published his drawings in the past, but he knew Susan would never approve. She had definite ideas about the life they would share and the career he should follow, and what she wanted for him was a military career that would keep them in the exciting whirl of Washington society. She was anxious that he complete this obligatory tour of duty on the frontier so they could return home.

Shields felt the train begin to slow down, and he glanced up to look out the window. He saw a low adobe house and a boy with a dog watching the train pass by. After some vacant land dotted with desert vegetation of scrub weed, yucca, and saguaro cactus had crossed his field of vision, he saw a whole cluster of low, gray, simple buildings.

"Prescott," the conductor announced, moving through the car. "This is Prescott. We'll stop here for ten minutes."

Shields stood up and buttoned his tunic. It was his last clean uniform, and he had saved it for the day of his arrival.

* * *

At the east end of the station platform, a stagecoach sat waiting for the train. The six horses, accustomed to the sound of a train, stood quietly in their harness as the big engine puffed by, its bell ringing loudly and its wheels squealing in protest as the engineer began applying the brakes. Four cavalry soldiers sat on horseback near the stage. One of them leaned forward and patted his mount as it shied at the commotion.

On the driver's seat of the coach sat Kevin O'Braugh, smartly dressed in a fresh uniform. On his sleeve the three yellow chevrons pointing down and three rockers across the top of the chevrons specified that he was a sergeant major, the highest rank in the army below that of an officer. The yellow chevrons and the matching stripe that ran down his trouser legs proclaimed him to be a cavalryman.

Sitting on the box with O'Braugh was Emily Rourke. At thirty-seven Emily was still a red-haired beauty, despite the hard life she led in the West. Her soft, kind, gray-green eyes were flashing with curiosity. She strained forward to see who got off the train.

"Careful now, lass, or you'll be tumblin' off this contraption," O'Braugh warned her with a playful smile.

Emily leaned back and grinned at him. "It would be a laugh now if I fell off while it was sittin' still, wouldn't it?" she teased.

"Sergeant Major, there's a lieutenant gettin' off now," one of the soldiers said. "You reckon that's him?"

"Well, now, how many lieutenants do you think would be comin' to Prescott today?" O'Braugh asked the young soldier sarcastically. "Go and fetch the lad, point out his conveyance to him, and then get his luggage."

The soldier started to urge his horse forward, but O'Braugh called to him, "Get off the horse and walk, Private. You don't approach an officer who's on foot while you're on horseback."

"Yes, Sergeant Major," the soldier responded contritely. He swung down from his saddle and hurried along the platform toward the officer. O'Braugh watched as the two men exchanged salutes. Then the soldier directed the lieutenant to the stage and started toward the baggage car while the officer strode toward the coach.

"Oh, an' he's a fine-lookin' man, don't you think, Mrs. Rourke?" O'Braugh said, as he climbed down from the coach to greet the approaching officer. " 'Tis the spittin' image of Colonel Shields himself."

"Do you remember him as a boy?" Emily asked.

"Aye. I saw the lad once at a review. He was a tiny boy, but he was the apple of his father's eye," O'Braugh said, straightening his uniform and pulling himself to his full height.

"Sergeant Major, is this my transportation to Fort Verde?" Shields asked.

"Yes, sir," O'Braugh said, saluting the young officer. "You'll be travelin' the thirty-five miles in style, you will, sir."

"I see," Shields said as he returned the salute. Then he looked up at the woman sitting on top of the stagecoach. "Miss, would you please get down now? Sergeant Major, you should know better than to fraternize with your lady friends while waiting to escort an officer, especially in front of the lower ranks."

"I beg your pardon, sir!" O'Braugh said firmly. "This is Mrs. Rourke, the owner of this stage. 'Tis she who'll be drivin' the lieutenant to the fort."

"I beg your forgiveness, madam," Shields said quickly, his face flushing in embarrassment.

"Don't fret over it, Lieutenant," Emily said easily. "Since my husband died, there's been more'n one man surprised at seein' me up here handlin' the ribbons. I'll give you a smooth enough ride."

"Lieutenant, 'tis proud I am to be servin' with you," O'Braugh said. "I was with your late father, an' though you don't remember me, I can recall meeting you when you were but a tyke."

"I see," Shields said, a subtle, chilly edge in his voice. He turned and saw the soldier approaching with his baggage. "I'll keep this with me," he said, reaching out and taking the portfolio from the struggling man. "The rest you can put in the boot."

"If you'd be anythin' akin to the colonel, lad, 'tis glad you are to be done with the fancy schoolin' and at your first postin'," O'Braugh went on, not noticing that Shields had cooled at his first mention of his father.

"Sergeant Major," Shields turned to face him and said brusquely, "my rank is lieutenant, not lad. And for your information, I find the fancy school, as you call it, far preferable to this godforsaken place."

"Aye, Lieutenant, I'll be rememberin' my place after this." O'Braugh lifted his head and stared off in the distance, stung by the sharp reprimand.

The soldier who had brought Shields's baggage from the train held the stagecoach door open for him. Once Shields was seated inside, O'Braugh climbed onto the box. Emily released the brake and snapped the whip, and the stage pulled away from the train station.

"Don't let it be gettin' you down," Emily said softly, sensing that O'Braugh was disappointed with the young lieutenant. "Don't forget, he's had a long, tirin' trip. Give him some time. And you'll have to admit, the first time a body sees this country, it's likely to set him back a bit." She laughed.

"Aye," O'Braugh said, joining in the laughter. "There ain't a thing growin' that don't prick, or a thing livin' that don't bite."

"He's certainly a fine-looking young man, with that dark hair and those gray eyes," Emily said. "And did you notice how neatly he was dressed? I'll just bet he broke all the ladies' hearts at the balls back East."

"Aye, it wouldn't surprise me," O'Braugh agreed.

Emily looked at him and smiled coquettishly. "Of course, bein' a handsome man yourself you'd be knowin' about these things."

"Mrs. Rourke!" O'Braugh gasped, reaching up to tug nervously at his collar.

Emily laughed and snapped the whip over the team, urging them to a brisk trot. "Tell me about Colonel Shields. Was he as good an officer as they say?"

"I've been in this army now for nearly thirty years," O'Braugh said, his brown eyes softening, "and the colonel was the finest officer I ever knew. Your own husband, Patrick, bless him, said the same thing. We were both in the same regiment then. 'Twas where Sergeant Rourke and I began our servin' together."

Emily nodded her head. "Patrick used to tell me some fine stories of things the two of you did together."

"Sure an' I hope he didn't tell you everything, now," O'Braugh said, teasing her.

"I know a few secrets about you, Kevin O'Braugh, secrets I'll not be tellin'." Emily cocked her head and laughed.

Then she looked back toward the coach. "Don't be too hard on the young man," she said. " 'Twould be hard for anyone to live up to his father's reputation. Give him time. I have a good feelin' about him."

O'Braugh smiled and reached over to take Emily's hand in his. "It's good instincts you've got, Emily Rourke," he said, squeezing her hand. "If you're speakin' for the lad, I'll give him all the time he needs."

Twenty miles away from the stage, a group of riders worked their way through a system of twisting canyons, avoiding the crests of hills so they would not be seen.

They called themselves the People, but to nearly everyone in their world they were known simply as the Enemy. For years the ancient Apache had made a prolonged, desperate effort to drive the Spanish, the Mexicans, and finally the Americans out of their ancestral lands. Then, in the winter of 1872, General George Crook had conducted a savage campaign against the Tonto Apache, killing several hundred and breaking the back of the organized resistance.

The peace plan that was drawn up afterward called for placing all of the Apache under four areas of control, one of which was headquartered at Fort Verde, in central Arizona. Although most of the Apache had reluctantly accepted the white ways, many did not like them. They neither knew how nor cared to cooperate, and they began to break out of the control areas to kill and raid as they had in the days before the peace plan. In the eastern part of the territory, a medicine man named Noch-ay-del-Klinne had led a band of warriors against soldiers and white settlers until he was killed. Further south it was Goyathlay, better known as Geronimo, who asserted the tribal ways of the People. But in central Arizona it was Manitoro who led a band of warriors on raids against the whites.

Now, as Manitoro and his men snaked through the canyons, he held up his hand to stop the others. Then, bending low to avoid making a silhouette, he moved to the crest of the hill. He was dark, handsome, and considerably taller than most other Apache, who tended to be short, muscular men. His black hair shone from frequent applications of animal grease, and his unusual cobalt-blue eyes were cold as they assessed the ranch house he was about to attack. He had sent two scouts ahead, and now he saw them coming back to give their report.

Manitoro slipped back to his warriors and greeted the returning scouts. "Were you seen?" he asked.

"No. The whites expect nothing."

"Good. This will be an easy fight," the leader said confidently.

"How is this battle to be fought?" one of the warriors asked.

"You have scouted the ranch carefully?" Manitoro asked the two scouts.

"Yes."

"Draw a picture of it then," he instructed the two men.

One of the scouts scratched a picture in the dirt, while the other looked over his shoulder to add details and make comments, until the entire layout was drawn. Manitoro looked at it, identifying the main house, the outbuildings, and all the major features of the place. He studied it for a long moment before he spoke.

"I will send two men here," he said, indicating on the impromptu map a spot on the opposite side of the ranch from where they were now hidden. "They will both have rifles. They will shoot and yell and make the whites think there are many. Then, when the whites are prepared to defend against an attack from that direction, we will attack from here." Manitoro put his fingers in both places, showing that the actual attack would come from the rear.

One of the scouts laughed. "Yes," he said. "That's a good plan. When do we attack?"

Manitoro pointed to the sky. "When the sun is there," he said. "It will then be behind our two men, and the whites will be blinded."

"Ha!" one of the men laughed, and he closed his eyes as if blinded by a bright light. "Where are you, *injuns*? Where are you? We cannot see you." He flailed his arms in front of him as if he were blind, and the others laughed at his antics.

"We will eat now," Manitoro ordered firmly, interrupting the clowning. "We will eat and wait for the sun to be our friend." The little war party moved down into an arroyo, where they purposely ate cold food, knowing that smoke from a fire would give away their position.

For the Apache the time before a battle was traditionally

a time for quiet and reflection. At such times Manitoro knew there was always the danger that his men might lose their courage and conviction. He had learned that it was best to talk then, to prevent their thinking of what lay ahead. In the old days, when there had been large war parties, the Gan dancers and medicine men had worked magic spells and told of the future, promising a good fight and a great victory.

There were no Gan dancers now, so Manitoro spoke to his men to fulfill the job once performed by the medicine men. He was known among the People as a man with the ability to see into the future. On many occasions he had shown this amazing ability, and now his men crowded around him and asked him to speak of what was going to be.

Breathing deeply with his eyes closed, Manitoro sat quietly for several minutes and let his mind drift. It was as if he were on the shore of a large lake, and part of him remained ashore and part of him floated out on the water. He could be in both places at once, and he could see one of his entities from the vantage point of the other. When he transferred his thoughts to the body that had drifted forward, he could look back and see himself still sitting quietly on the shore. But he could also look around and see events that had not yet happened. It was in this way that he could tell the future.

"Now, listen," he spoke softly to his men from his trance-like state. "Do not fear the battle we are about to fight, for we will have victory, and their horses and their cattle and all that we want will be ours."

The warriors smiled broadly and poked each other as they thought of the easy victory before them.

Suddenly Manitoro's mind filled with another image— the image of a man dressed in blue. He was a tall man, as tall as Manitoro. His eyes were pale gray, the color of the sky just before a storm. In the image before him, Manitoro saw the man stick his hand into a fire and draw back a drink of cool water. He did not know how such a feat could be done, and the image disturbed him so deeply that he willed his two entities to return to one.

"It is time," someone was saying. Startled, Manitoro looked at the speaker and realized that the brave had repeated the sentence many times. He closed his eyes and pressed his fingers against his eyelids to clear the lingering vision from his mind.

"Yes," he said. He stood up and started toward his horse. "It is time."

A few minutes later, as planned, two warriors moved stealthily around to the other side of the ranch house. Concealed among the rocks, yet able to observe the scene below, Manitoro waited until they were in position. Then with a wave of his hand he ordered a bowman to shoot an arrow across the space, the signal for the two warriors to begin their attack. He listened as the two warriors started shooting their rifles and yelling.

"It sounds as if there are twenty men," one of the warriors waiting next to Manitoro whispered.

Manitoro watched as the doors to the big house and the smaller ranch house opened. One man came from the big house, and five ran from the ranch house. All were carrying rifles, which they started firing toward the two warriors.

"Our trick has worked," Manitoro hissed triumphantly. "Let us attack!"

Manitoro slapped his legs against the sides of his horse, urging his animal forward. The group of ten warriors thundered down the side of the hill as if they were an attacking army.

"My God . . . they're all around us!" one of the white men yelled, seconds before an arrow pierced his neck.

"Ayiieee! Such a shot!" one of the Indians yelled proudly.

Manitoro and his group swept through the little band of defenders firing rifles, pistols, and bows and arrows. It was a short, bloody battle and was over within a few minutes.

"Those who do not have rifles take these," Manitoro shouted, pointing to the weapons of the dead men. "Let us go in the house!"

Manitoro was the first one inside. He saw a woman sitting on the floor leaning against the wall. Her eyes were open wide, and she was staring at him defiantly. Manitoro shot her without a word and then looked through the rest of the house. He found no one else, but as he was leaving he smelled something cooking. He walked over to the stove, opened the oven, and pulled out a sheet of cookies—cinnamon cookies. As he held one under his nose he felt a strange dizziness and a deep, dark awareness. He looked down at the woman he had just killed, and then at the tray of cookies she had baked. He raised one to his mouth, but he found he could not eat it.

"Ah, look," one of his warriors said as he entered the house at that moment. "The woman knew we were coming and cooked for us." He grabbed a cookie and stuffed it in his mouth, smiling at his joke. Manitoro went out onto the porch and gulped a few deep breaths of fresh air, and the dizziness passed.

When he and his raiding party returned to the war camp just before dark, they were greeted by several dozen men and women. Like Geronimo, Manitoro was called a renegade by the whites. And, like Geronimo, Manitoro had a large following, almost as large as the main group under Chief Chatoma, the ancestral head of the Tonto. Chief Chatoma had chosen the way of peace, and Manitoro felt only disgust when he thought of the impotent old man and the squaw-men who were with him.

"It was a great victory," one of the raiders bragged to the others. He held up the rifle he had taken. "See how many guns we have?"

"Yes, and look at the horses. We have a string of fine horses," one of the others boasted.

"I would have gone," complained a brave who had remained in the camp. "You left before light, and I didn't hear you. I would have gone."

Manitoro laughed. "It is all right," he said. "We will go again. There is a place where the white man's stagecoach stops to change horses. We will attack there before the sun sets tonight."

"You would make two battles in one day?" one of the warriors asked in surprise. "Ayiiee, I think no one has ever done this before."

Manitoro smiled and put his thumb to his chest. "There has never been a Manitoro before," he said. "The grandchildren of our grandchildren will sing songs of Manitoro."

Half a dozen Indian maidens were clustered around Manitoro, offering him food and water and, by extension, themselves. Manitoro pointed to one of them. "You," he said. "When I return, you will be with me."

"I am pleased that you have chosen me," the maid said, smiling happily at him and triumphantly at the other maidens.

At the ranch Manitoro had just attacked, one man had escaped the slaughter and was left alive. Ben Crabtree had been in the privy when the Indians attacked and, trapped in the middle of the battlefield without a weapon, he had had no choice but to stay inside and hope that the Indians would not take too close a look. Trembling in fear, he had peeked through the cracks in the simple plank structure and watched as the Apache rode down behind the defenders, firing with deadly accuracy. The horrible battle, if it could be called that, was over within moments. He watched as the Indians took the guns from the bodies and then went into the house. Seconds after they entered the house, he heard a shot and knew that Mrs. Webb must have been killed.

The Apache also checked the bunkhouse and the barn. When one of them started toward the privy, Ben opened the seat bench and lowered himself into the pit with the night soil. The smell was awful, but the Indian who was looking did no more than open the door and peer inside. The smell, which was nearly asphyxiating to Ben, was enough to drive the Indian away without making a more thorough search.

After the Indians had left, Ben went down to the horse trough and bathed. He was not concerned about fouling the water for the horses . . . there were no horses left. Nor chickens. Nor eggs. The chickens the Indians had taken with them, tied across their saddles; the eggs they had eaten on the spot, breaking the shells and swallowing them raw.

Ben had been working at the ranch for only two weeks, so he did not know the Webbs very well, but they had been decent people to work for, so he felt awful about what had happened. Not that there was anything he could have done; had he left the privy, he would have been killed like the others. This way, at least, he would be able to tell someone what had happened. If they ever caught the redskins who did it, Ben Crabtree would be able to identify them—especially the tall bastard with the dark blue eyes.

Chapter Two

The stagecoach Mark Shields was riding in was big, well sprung, and remarkably well maintained. The leather seats were clean, and the one or two tears he noticed had been expertly sewn. Shields wondered if the stage was always this spotless or if extra effort had been made to clean it for his benefit. Almost as soon as the thought struck him, he realized what a vanity such an idea was. *Why would a private coach company clean the stage just for the arrival of a second lieutenant in the U.S. Army?* he asked himself laughingly. He decided that Mrs. Rourke must be a woman of character and industry.

Outside the coach, the desert and mountain panorama slid past his window. The stagecoach was moving rather briskly, and the wheels threw up little rooster tails of dirt that hung in the air, marking their passage down the road. Above him, he could hear the whistle and the pop of the whip as Emily Rourke urged her team on. She was, he decided, exceptionally skilled at her job. Though driving a stage was usually a man's job, she was in no way masculine. She was an unusually attractive woman, a fact he was sure the sergeant had noticed as well.

Although Sergeant O'Braugh had appeared eager to speak of Shields's father, the lieutenant had discouraged it immediately. In fact, Shields realized that he had been rather short with the sergeant. Shields was not insensitive and did not enjoy hurting O'Braugh's feelings, but he was not his father, and he did not want to be compared to his father any longer.

19

It was enough to justify the expectations of command put on him by his commission from West Point. It would be impossible to measure up to the reputation his father enjoyed. In fact, though he had never mentioned it to anyone for fear of being misunderstood, Shields was not at all sure that his father, were he alive today, could even live up to his own reputation. Tales of Colonel Benjaman Shields had taken on larger-than-life proportions in the years since his father's heroic death.

Brushing thoughts of his father aside, Mark Shields studied the escort detail that accompanied the coach. The detail consisted of four privates: two men who always rode close to the stage and two who rode within sight of the coach, though they were sometimes as far as a mile away. He realized then that they must be passing through territory that was frequently subjected to Indian attack and that Sergeant O'Braugh was deploying his men in the classic maneuver for protecting the flank while on the march in hostile territory. Shields felt he was seeing a chapter of his textbook come to life, and, despite himself, he felt a thrill of excitement. This was not an exercise at West Point; this was the real thing!

The coach started up a long climb, and Shields could feel the horses straining in the harness as they negotiated the grade. When they finally reached the top, the stage stopped, and O'Braugh jumped down and opened the door of the coach.

"Lieutenant Shields, we'll be givin' the horses a bit of a blow here. You can stretch your legs if you're of a mind."

"Thank you," Shields replied. "I would like to walk around a little."

Shields walked over to the edge of the road and looked out. From where he stood there was a commanding view of ochre and burnt-umber hills, and he could see for several breathtakingly beautiful miles. As he scanned the awesome vista, he noticed a little plume of smoke that rose like a rope from the horizon. Puzzled, he frowned and stared at it for a long moment.

"I see you've noticed it, sir," O'Braugh said, walking over to stand beside Shields.

"Is it Indians?"

"It's too big for a campfire," O'Braugh replied, shaking his head.

"Maybe it's a brush fire."

"Aye, it could be that. Or it could be worse."

"What do you mean?" Shields asked as he turned to look at O'Braugh.

"There's a ranch over that way, belongs to a fella named Webb. He an' his wife are nice folks, and they've got some nice people workin' for 'em. I wouldn't want to think they're havin' trouble."

"Sergeant, could that fire be the work of this Indian fellow, Manitoro, I've been hearing about?"

"Yes, sir, it could be," O'Braugh said. He looked back toward the horses. "If you've had your stretch, sir, and with your permission, I think we'd best be getting on."

"Carry on, Sergeant," Shields said as if giving the orders, when in fact he was merely following Sergeant Major O'Braugh's suggestion.

Captain Alan Ross stood in the shade of the sally port between the commanding officer's quarters and the headquarters building at Fort Verde. Shielded from the sun and constructed in such a way as to create a breeze, the sally port was cool and pleasant. Actually, it was not that unpleasant in the buildings, for they were cooled by olla jars, large clay pots filled with water and suspended from the ceiling. The evaporation of the water created a type of air-conditioning, a trick that the Army of the Southwest had learned from the Mexicans, who had learned it from the Indians many years earlier.

On the hot, dusty parade ground, a drill was in progress. Two dozen soldiers were listlessly dismounting, assembling, then disassembling a Gatling gun, and then remounting and doing the same thing all over again. He could hear the grating of metal on metal as the components were clicked into place, mingled with the shouted orders of the drill sergeants and the curses of the sweating men. It was, Captain Ross decided, like nearly everything else in the accursed Army of the Southwest—a complete and total waste of time. Captain Ross had never seen a Gatling gun used in action against the Indians, nor did he know of any incident when the weapon had actually been used. The guns were too cumbersome to take along and unsuited to the fluid movement of battle against the Indians. But it was considered a lack of discipline to allow the soldiers simply to lie around the barracks all day with no duty. Thus the days became an endless procession of drills, parades, and stable detail.

"Cap'n, sir, the mornin' report is ready for your signature," the company clerk called through the open top half of the Dutch door that led into the orderly room.

Captain Ross ran his hand through his white hair and looked toward the clerk. The young man, who could not be more than twenty years old, had not even been born when Captain Ross received his commission. Now, over twenty years later, Alan Ross was stuck in the rank of captain, while his contemporaries were lieutenant colonels and full colonels. He did not think it was mere oversight that kept him down. He truly believed he had enemies in high places, friends and supporters of Custer who had disapproved of his reports and statements to the press after the Custer massacre. This belief sustained him, for he could not accept that there might be some other reason for his condition.

"Did you put the new lieutenant on the morning report?" Captain Ross asked his clerk.

"No, sir."

"Why not?"

"Well, sir, he ain't here," the clerk explained. "And the first sergeant, he said I ought not to put him on till he gets here."

"Who's running this fort, Private? The first sergeant or me?" Captain Ross asked sternly.

"You are, sir," the private replied contritely.

"Then you do what I say," Captain Ross reminded him.

"Yes, sir."

Ross waited until the clerk had gone back into the orderly room. Then, when he was certain that he was alone and no one was watching him, he reached his hand down into one of the olla jars that hung over the sally port and removed from it a bottle of whiskey. He pulled the cork and took several long, deep swallows and then brought the bottle down with a loud, satisfied exhalation of breath. He ran the back of his hand across his mouth, corked the bottle, and put it back in the olla jar.

Once again Ross mulled over his career and his rank. With the new lieutenant on his roster, he would have as many officers under him as a lieutenant colonel. Headquar-

ters would have to notice that, and surely they would have to
promote him soon.

Of course, his count included Dr. Hartfield, and techni-
cally the doctor was not listed on the muster of officers. As a
major, Dr. Hartfield actually outranked Ross. But, since he
was a doctor, he had no command function, and that meant
Ross was the senior officer on post.

James Hartfield was married, and his wife, Amy, lived
on the post with him. There were half a dozen wives at the
fort, though Mrs. Hartfield was the only officer's wife. The
other ladies were married to sergeants.

Ross had never been married. He did not believe an
officer should be married, since he believed marriage inter-
fered with the performance of duty. He once made that very
comment to Dr. Hartfield, only to have Hartfield reply that a
wife was less of an interference to an officer's career than
whiskey. The remark had angered Ross, and if anyone else
had said it, Ross would have had him up on charges of
insubordination. He could not do that with Hartfield, however, because even though the doctor could have no command, Hartfield still outranked him.

A door opened nearby, and Ross looked across the parade ground to see Amy Hartfield walk from her house to the
pump to draw a bucket of water. Concealed in the protective
shadows of the sally port, Ross stared at her. Her soft brown
hair neatly framed her face, and her blue dress matched the
color of her eyes. Her trim form moved gracefully as she
performed her task. She was a very handsome woman, and
he often wondered why such a pretty woman would marry a
man as homely as Dr. Hartfield.

Amy Hartfield returned to her kitchen with the bucket
of water and put it on the shelf next to the dipper. The
building she and her husband lived in was both their home
and the fort hospital, and from the kitchen she could look
across the center hallway into the hospital section. She could
see her husband in there now, tending to the half dozen
soldiers who had reported on sick call. She knew he was
caring for two men with broken bones, one man with a case
of measles, and three men with undetermined maladies who
would probably be returned to duty. Her husband had two

orderlies working with him. When he looked up and saw her, he smiled and left the hospital ward to speak with her.

As he approached, Amy felt a warming glow flush her cheeks. He was as handsome today as he was when she had married him twenty years ago. Whenever she mentioned it to him, he would laughingly remind her that this was certainly a case of handsomeness being in the eyes of the beholder.

He was fairly short, perhaps five feet six, and he certainly had thickened around the middle. *He enjoys my cooking—that's evident!* Amy thought with a twinge of pride. His light hair was thin, and his pale blue eyes peered at her from behind wire-rimmed glasses. Yet this simple man radiated a warmth, compassion, and deep love for her that made him very handsome to Amy. She felt she was extremely lucky to have such a husband and was unaware that other men found her pretty.

Hartfield took the dipper from the shelf and scooped out a drink of water. "Have you heard anything new about the arrival of our new officer?" he asked.

"Corporal Aikins said the coach should be here by noon," she answered.

Hartfield smiled. "I suppose you and the other ladies will have the post decorated for a dance by nightfall," he said knowingly.

"It is traditional," she insisted, "to welcome new officers with a dinner and a dance."

The doctor hung the dipper and turned to her. "Yes, on large forts where there are many officers' wives," he reminded her gently. "I think we would be forgiven if we didn't keep up the tradition here."

"Jimmy, we have been looking for a suitable excuse to have a dance, and we're going to do it," Amy insisted. Her pretty chin was set, and her blue eyes looked at him with determination.

Hartfield chuckled. He knew that his wife and the other women had been planning this party from the moment they learned a new officer would be coming to the post, and he knew nothing would make them change their plans now.

"Besides," she went on, "he'll soon be married, and then we'll really have something to celebrate. We shall have the wedding here. Oh, Jimmy, won't that be grand?"

Hartfield looked up. "Married, you say? How do you know that?"

"Mrs. Barnes told me. Her sister is married to a sergeant who is posted at West Point, and she said our new lieutenant is to marry a general's daughter, who is following him out here. She'll be arriving in a couple of weeks."

Hartfield shook his head and laughed.

"Don't you believe me?" Amy asked.

"Oh, yes, I believe you. I was just thinking about the power of gossip. If the army could figure out some way to harness the ability you women have to exchange information so quickly, they'd know everything they needed to know about the enemy well in advance, and they'd never lose a battle!"

The coach run between Prescott and Fort Verde passed over the Mazatzal Mountains, descending from the crests just before reaching the Verde River valley and Fort Verde. The stage drivers said that they did not drive into Fort Verde; they descended into it. Passengers could see Fort Verde as soon as the stage reached Eagle Pass, and it remained visible, like a toy fort with tin soldiers, as the stage wound its way down from the clouds that sometimes clung to the top of the mountain.

As if he were a passenger in a balloon, Shields was able to study the layout of the fort and compare it to the description that accompanied his orders.

"Established in January, 1864, the post was originally located on the west bank of the Rio Verde about thirty-five miles east of Prescott," the official description read. "Its purpose is to provide protection for ranchers, miners, and merchants in the district. It was moved in the spring of 1871 to a place one mile west of the Verde River, half a mile below the mouth of Beaver Creek. Originally named Camp Lincoln, the name has been changed to avoid confusion with Camp Lincoln, Dakota Territory, and has been redesignated Fort Verde.

"The structures of the post are built around a parade ground, two hundred feet long by one hundred fifty feet wide. The long sides lie north and south. The post stockade, post hospital and surgeon's quarters, post headquarters, and commanding officers' quarters are at the north end. The enlisted men's quarters and the laundresses' quarters are along the eastern side; the stables and barns are along the southern side; the sutler's store, the officers' quarters, and the parking area for wagons are on the west."

As the coach moved on, Shields enjoyed the unique perspective of the post from high above it. He could even see that a couple of men on stable detail were shirking their duty behind the barn.

The coach turned off the high road and began the descent into the post. Soon he felt it braking and knew that Mrs. Rourke was applying the lever. A moment later they were off the hill and moving onto the post. As they halted in front of the headquarters building, Shields looked out the window. After four years of schooling and over a week of travel, he was finally at his first posting. He took a deep breath and prepared to plunge in.

Shields reached for the door, but it was opened for him. Sergeant Major O'Braugh stood at attention beside the coach, his hand raised in a sharp military salute as Shields stepped down. Returning the salute, Shields then saw a white-haired man coming toward him. He was surprised to see that the man was only a captain, and he feared somewhere deep inside that this might be himself in twenty years.

Shields was so lost in his thoughts and impressions that he nearly forgot to report. He heard O'Braugh whisper to him, "Report to the commander, lad."

Clearing his throat, he saluted. "Second Lieutenant Mark Shields reporting, sir. I have a copy of my orders with me."

"Leave them with the clerk," Captain Ross said, returning the salute. "Welcome to Fort Verde," he said, offering his hand to Shields.

"Thank you, sir."

Ross gestured toward the headquarters building. "Come into my office, Lieutenant. It's cooler inside."

Once inside the office, Ross closed the door and strode to his desk in the center of the room. "I don't know what they told you about me back at West Point," Ross began, "but it would be better if you got all your information firsthand, don't you agree?"

"Yes, sir," Shields said, puzzled. In truth no one had ever told him a thing about Captain Ross. He had never heard of him until he had seen the name on his orders.

"I know there's talk about me back East," Ross went on. "There's a conspiracy to keep me a captain forever, probably because of the Custer thing. Well, I don't care. There is such a thing as honor, you know, and I would rather be an honorable captain than a colonel or general who has compromised his honor."

"Yes, sir, I quite agree," Shields said, though he had no idea what Captain Ross was talking about.

"I don't want you to get the wrong idea," Ross said as he took a bottle of whiskey from a cabinet near his desk and, still standing, poured them each a glass. "Ordinarily, I don't hold with my officers drinking on duty, but the arrival of a new lieutenant calls for a drink." He held the glass out. Shields took it, though it seemed a little early in the day to him, duty or no.

"To the Republic," Ross said, holding his glass up.

"To the Republic, sir," Shields repeated, touching his glass to the commander's. He tossed the liquid down, feeling its fire burn him. He fought hard against coughing.

"I was with General Terry, you know," Ross went on. "I was the one who found Custer and his men." A distant light flashed in the captain's eyes, and he poured himself another drink, then tossed it down as if it were water. "The bodies lay swollen and stinking in the sun," he said. "Vultures were going to work where the Indians left off—plucking out eyes, cleaning the bones. I yelled at them to frighten them away, and one of them flew over me carrying a long piece of entrail." Ross shivered and poured himself a third glass, tossing it down as easily as he had the first two. "I . . . I shot at it, and it dropped the entrail . . . on me." Unthinkingly he rubbed at his tunic as if to brush the gruesome item away. "I never could get that shirt clean after that. I just threw it away." He poured himself a fourth drink.

Shields stood there wondering what he should do next. There was a moment of uncomfortable silence, then the distant light left Ross's eyes.

"It could have all been prevented, you know. If General Terry had listened to me, had given me the command I'd asked for, we would have arrived on the field of battle before Custer."

"But, sir, in that case it might have been you lying on that field," Shields suggested.

"No, I wouldn't have made the same blunders. Custer was a fool. When I said so in my report, I was censured. He still has his supporters, even today, you know, and they are conspiring against me, keeping me down." He poured himself a fifth drink. "I know you've heard stories about me—I know they talk about me back East. But I thought you might rather hear the truth."

There was a knock on the door, and Ross called out. "Enter."

A short, round man wearing the uniform and insignia of a major in the medical corps stepped inside. "I wanted to greet the new lieutenant," he said, smiling at Shields.

"Yes, well, I've got work to do. Perhaps you can show him around the post," Ross said. As he took a step, he stumbled and had to catch himself.

"I'm Dr. Hartfield," the doctor said. "I'm a major, but since I have no command function around here, please feel free to call me Jim. Come on, I'll show you the place."

"Thank you," Shields said. He looked back over his shoulder as they left the headquarters building.

"You're concerned about Ross?" Jim Hartfield asked.

"No, sir," Shields said quickly. "I wouldn't presume to . . ." He let the sentence drop.

"You wouldn't presume to call him a drunk?" When Shields did not answer, Hartfield went on. "He is a drunk," he said simply. "I'm not condemning him for it. I don't think medical science understands all there is to be known about addiction to spirits. To society it's clearly a question of weak moral fiber, but I believe there is more to it than that. I believe drunkenness is a disease." He shook his head. "The medical profession, the legal profession, and of course the clergy all insist that it's a deficiency of character. I only know that if that's so, there must be a major problem with the way the army selects its soldiers, for drunkenness is rampant and is no respecter of rank. It affects officers as well as the enlisted men."

"I suppose if anyone has a right to be a drunk, Captain Ross has," Shields said.

"He told you about finding Custer's men?"

"Yes, sir."

"That's a specter that would haunt any man, I agree,"

the doctor said. He pointed to a row of tiny, one-room cabins. "Here are the officers' quarters."

"Where do the married officers live?"

Hartfield smiled. "I'm the only one who is married, and I live in the surgeon's quarters, attached to the hospital. Ross is the post commander, so he lives in the big house there, even though he isn't married. I heard you were about to be married."

Shields looked at the surgeon in surprise.

"You wonder how I know." The doctor laughed. "Well, Lieutenant, such news travels through the women on military posts with the speed of light. Anyway, married or single, you'll live in one of these cabins. Don't worry, though, Amy and some of the other women will have it fixed up just fine by the time your lady arrives. Fact is, I'm sure they'll tell you all about it tonight."

"Tonight?"

"Yes. They've planned a party in your honor."

"Oh, I wish they hadn't gone to such trouble," Shields protested.

"Don't flatter yourself, Lieutenant, it has nothing to do with you. It's just an excuse to have one, that's all," he said, chuckling.

"Dr. Hartfield! Dr. Hartfield!" someone shouted. Shields turned to see a soldier running across the parade ground. "The patrol just brought in a wounded ranch hand!"

In the post surgery a group of men had gathered around Ben Crabtree. A patrol had found him, injured and walking on the trail to the post. He had left the Webb ranch on foot and, running, had fallen, breaking his arm. While Dr. Hartfield tended to him, he told the men about the Indian attack, about the slaughter of the Webbs and the other hands, and about his survival by hiding in the privy. "I went through all that, then fell on the trail like a dumb tenderfoot," he groaned.

One of those listening to Crabtree's story was Farley Branson, the civilian manager of the sutler's store. Tall and darkly handsome, with a well-trimmed goatee, Branson was very agitated by the story Ben Crabtree told.

"Captain Ross, surely now you agree with me when I say you should call out the troops. Call out the entire post, sir, and punish the Indians."

"Punish which Indians?" Ross replied.

"Any of them or all of them," Branson said. "It doesn't matter. Don't you see? The only thing these Indians understand is force. You should run all of them out of here, move them onto the reservation down at San Carlos."

"Branson, you don't really mean that," Dr. Hartfield said, looking at the sutler sternly. "Chatoma and his bunch are good citizens."

"They are Indians, and they are providing a safe haven for Manitoro and his kind."

"Do you believe that, Sergeant Major?" Dr. Hartfield asked O'Braugh.

"No, sir," O'Braugh answered, shaking his head.

"I don't either," the doctor said disgustedly.

"Still," Ross said, holding up his hand, "there may be something to what Mr. Branson suggests."

"Captain Ross, what are you saying?" Hartfield demanded. "That you agree with Branson? That you believe Chatoma and his bunch should be punished for what Manitoro is doing?"

"As far as I know, Chatoma is a decent Indian," Ross said. "But Mr. Branson may be right when he says that the Indians who are doing this can return to Chatoma's camp and know that we won't attack them."

"You're gonna get some good with the bad," Branson said, pleased to have Ross agree with him. He pressed his argument further. "But if you'd attack Chatoma's camp one time, you'd bring all of them into line."

"Lieutenant Macklin," Ross said, seeing the man standing in the group clustered around Crabtree.

"Yes, sir?" answered a slender, blond-haired, blue-eyed man.

"Lieutenant, I want you to get a detail of men together. Get ready to march."

"Yes, sir."

"That's more like it," Branson said, a pleased smile spreading over his face.

"This isn't a punishment detail, Mr. Branson," Ross said. "I'm merely sending a detail out to the Webb ranch."

"What do I do there, sir?" Macklin asked.

"Have a look around," Ross ordered. "And bury the bodies."

"Yes, sir."

"Captain Ross," Shields put in quickly. "Have I your permission to accompany the lieutenant on his mission?"

Ross looked at Shields, and for a moment Shields thought he could see the distant light again. "You know what you're letting yourself in for?"

"Yes, sir," Shields replied.

"All right," Ross agreed. "The sooner you get broken in, the sooner you'll be of some use. You can go."

"Lieutenant Macklin, you'll be needin' a sergeant, sir," O'Braugh said.

"Yes. Would you find one for me?" Macklin said.

"'Tis myself that'll be goin'," O'Braugh volunteered.

"Very well. Assemble the men, Sergeant Major. Every man is to be armed with a carbine and forty rounds of ammunition. We'll leave in five minutes."

"Aye, sir."

"Shields, come with me. I'll help you select a mount," Macklin offered.

"Thank you," Shields answered. He looked back at the doctor, who was just finishing with Ben Crabtree's arm. "Doctor, you'll give my apologies to the ladies? I'm afraid I won't be able to join them tonight."

"I'll tell them," the doctor said. "You just be careful on that patrol so you're around to celebrate your arrival sometime later."

Chapter Three

The entire fort turned out for the departure of the patrol. The officers and men who were not part of the patrol had been temporarily relieved of their duties to form a regimental parade around the quadrangle. Shields was on horseback, standing in his stirrups, in the absolute silence that hung over the three hundred people assembled in the parade ground. The only sound that could be heard was the snapping and flapping of the garrison flag, flying high overhead.

Shields surveyed the assembled patrol, a dozen mounted cavalrymen stretched out in a long single line facing Lieutenant Macklin, the officer in charge, and Sergeant Major O'Braugh.

"Sergeant O'Braugh, prepare to move out!" Macklin shouted.

"Troop, form column of twos!" O'Braugh yelled, his strong command voice echoing across the parade ground.

The men executed the command.

"Guidon, post!" O'Braugh shouted, and a soldier carrying a red and white pennant galloped to the head of the column.

"Sir," O'Braugh said, saluting Macklin. "The troop is formed."

"Move them out," Macklin commanded.

O'Braugh stood high in his stirrups. "Forward, ho!" he yelled.

As the troop rode across the parade ground, Shields looked over at the stagecoach he had ridden in on. Mrs.

Rourke was sitting on the seat watching the men leave, and
he thought he could detect more than a casual interest in the
way she watched Sergeant O'Braugh. When she saw that
Shields was looking at her, she waved. Military decorum
prevented him from returning her wave, but he did nod in
acknowledgment of her greeting.

The column moved at a steady, rapid pace. The Arizona
desert stretched out before them in folds of hills, one after
another. As each ridge was crested there was another, then
another still. After they had been on the trail for an hour,
Lieutenant Macklin held up his hand to bring the column to a
halt and said, "Sergeant, we'll dismount and walk the horses
for ten minutes."

"Yes, sir," O'Braugh replied, and he passed on the order
to the men and then dismounted himself.

Shields had bought an excellent pair of binoculars when
he graduated from West Point, and he now took them out of
the case and began scanning the horizon. He saw only dusty
rocks, shimmering desert grass, and more ranges of hills
under the beating sun.

"Good-looking glasses," Macklin observed.

"Would you like to look through them?" Shields offered.

"Yes, thank you." Macklin took the glasses and swept the
horizon with them, then handed them back. "So," he said.
"What do you think of it out here?"

"It's, uh, quite overwhelming," Shields said.

Macklin laughed. "That's a polite way of putting it," he
said. "Of course, you're still new here. I've been here five
years."

"Five years?" Shields's heart sank. He had expected that
a three-year posting was the maximum length of time.

"Five long, lonely years," he said. Then his eyes bright-
ened, and he smiled. "But I only have two months to go, and
my tour of duty is over."

"Where will you go then?"

"I'm going back to Ohio," he said. "I was a fool to ever
leave in the first place. I hear you have a sweetheart, and
you're bringing her out here."

"Does no one out here have a respect for privacy?"
Shields protested, shaking his head.

Macklin laughed. "Privacy? No, I'm afraid not. There's

little enough to do, so everyone makes everyone else's business his own."

"I don't like that," Shields complained.

"You may as well get used to it. It's a way of life," Macklin said. Then he turned and called to O'Braugh, "Sergeant, get the men mounted."

"Yes, sir," O'Braugh replied.

The patrol rode through the dusty hills of Arizona Territory for two more hours before Shields noticed the circling birds. At first the sight meant nothing to him, just another new phenomenon to absorb. But he noticed that the men had become strangely uneasy and sullen. He asked Sergeant O'Braugh about it.

"Have you not seen vultures before, sir?" O'Braugh asked.

With a hollow sensation in the pit of his stomach, Shields then knew what it was. They were approaching the ranch, and the vultures were already at work on the bodies.

About ten minutes later the patrol crested the last rise, and they were able to look down into the little valley where the ranch lay. A blackened pile of rubble told where the main house once stood. The privy where Ben Crabtree had hidden, the barn, and the bunkhouse were still intact. Shields realized then that the smoke he had seen this morning had come from this fire. He was sickened at the thought that while he had been watching from a distance, safe and comfortable, men were dying.

"There they are, sir," O'Braugh said to Macklin. He pointed to something black and moving on the ground. For an instant Shields had no idea what it was; then it dawned on him that he was watching a cluster of vultures. What was under the birds he did not particularly want to see.

"Forward at a trot, Sergeant," Macklin ordered.

The column broke into a trot at O'Braugh's command. Sabers, canteens, mess kits, and carbines jangled under the irregular rhythm of the trotting horses, and dust boiled up behind them. They held the trot until they were within a hundred yards of the ranch.

"At a gallop!" Macklin called. He stood in his stirrups and drew his saber, pointing it forward. The saber was not drawn as a weapon but as a means of signaling the next command. A drawn saber meant that carbines should be pulled from the saddle scabbard and held at the ready.

Every nerve in Shields's body tingled as the group of soldiers swept down on the ranch. He was alert to every blade of grass, every rock and stone, every hill and gully.

When they had reached the ranch, Macklin ordered them to halt. "Line of skirmishers, front and rear," he called, and two squads moved into position.

As Macklin swung down from his horse, Shields started to dismount, too.

"No, Shields," Macklin said, holding up his hand. "The regulations say that when a party is on scout in a suspicious area, the commander and the second in command should never dismount at the same time unless forming a defensive perimeter."

"Yes, sir," Shields said, his cheeks flushing with embarrassment. He knew that as well as he knew his own name, but he had forgotten it in the tension of his very first assignment.

At Lieutenant Macklin's direction, the soldiers took aim and fired at the vultures. Three of the big black birds were hit. They lay on the dusty ground flapping their wings as the others flew away, exposing the bodies of the rancher and his men. Shields gasped when he saw them. He looked at the one nearest him. The body was stripped naked. The top of the head was open, and brains spilled onto the ground. The man's penis and testicles had been cut away.

Shields turned away and fought hard to keep himself from throwing up. One of the wounded vultures flapped its way along the ground, finally dying just a few feet away from him. Shields could see the blood on the bird's beak. He thought of the story Captain Ross had told him and could understand what it had been like to happen upon a battlefield strewn with hundreds of bodies that looked just like this.

"Sergeant, form a burial detail," Macklin ordered.

O'Braugh issued the orders, and six men began digging graves while the others stayed on alert. Macklin remounted and rode over to Shields. He offered him a bottle.

"No," Shields said, waving it away. "Thanks, anyway."

Macklin took a drink and then put the bottle away.

"You're just as well to turn it down," he said. "I have to confess, taking a drink doesn't make it any easier."

"Do you . . . do you see things like this often?"

"More often than I'd like," Macklin said. "Though it's not a sight you run into every day. It's worse when there're women and children."

"There are none here?"

"They found what's left of the woman in the house," Macklin said. "The Webbs didn't have any children."

"Did you know them?"

"Sure. I danced with Mrs. Webb at the Christmas ball last year. She was a pretty woman."

A few minutes later the burial was completed. Macklin told the sergeant to have the men remount. "If we push it," he said to Shields, "we can be back at the fort before midnight."

Shields twisted around in his saddle as they rode away, looking back at the little mounds they were leaving behind them. Somehow what they did seemed inappropriate. There was no service of any kind, no mourners, no preacher, just a dozen soldiers who sweated and panted as they dug the holes, dropped the bodies in, and left.

"You're thinking we should've done more," Macklin said. When Shields looked at him in surprise, Macklin smiled in understanding. "I know, because I remember my first time. But, Shields, remember this. There are thousands of lonely graves all over the West, and those who were buried are the lucky ones. Thousands more died God only knows where. Their bones were picked clean by the vultures and scattered by the coyotes. Death, like life, is harsh out here."

Macklin had barely finished the statement when Shields heard a whistling sound, followed by a thunk that sounded like a man slapping a piece of canvas. He turned to see a little puff of dust fly up from Macklin's tunic, then a squirt of blood streaming from a large hole. Macklin let out a little sound, a gagging cough that died in his throat, and fell from his horse.

Shields heard the rifle fire and the whizzing sound of a bullet flying past his ear. He wondered why he had not heard the rifle shot that hit Macklin. He started to dismount to look at Macklin, but Sergeant O'Braugh grabbed him by the arm and lifted him back to the saddle.

"We've no time, Lieutenant," O'Braugh shouted. "Look!"

Snapping his head around, his eyes following O'Braugh's outstretched arm, Shields saw a long line of warriors racing down the hill toward them. Without counting them, he in-

stantly knew that there were easily three times more Indians
than there were soldiers. In that same sweeping glance,
Shields spotted a commanding warrior, taller than the others,
who was clearly their leader. *Manitoro?* he wondered.

Shields glanced down at Macklin and saw that his eyes
were open and glazed. He was not moving, and Shields was
sure he was dead.

"He's gone! You're in command!" O'Braugh shouted
desperately.

There was no way to go except back in the direction they
had just come.

"Back to the ranch!" Shields ordered, and the soldiers,
grateful that Shields had assumed command, started back at a
gallop.

"The two men in the rear!" Shields shouted. "Fire at the
Indians, then advance to the front so the next two can fire.
Maintain that pattern. Keep that up, and we'll always have
someone covering us."

The two rear-most troopers twisted in their saddles and
fired at the pursuing Indians. One of the Indians dropped
from his pony. The soldiers who had fired galloped to the
front of the column, and the next two troopers in line fired.
Though neither of them scored a hit, they did force the
Indians to keep their distance.

Shields stayed toward the rear of his detail, seeing to it
that they kept firing steadily.

They quickly reached the ranch. Shields rapidly studied
the area, looking for a good position that would offer some
cover. There was a small berm of ground around the root
cellar, and it would provide some protection.

"There!" he shouted, pointing.

Under his direction the patrol reached the cover of the
root cellar. Dismounting quickly, they hurled themselves to
the ground and rapidly opened fire on the attacking Indians.
Protected by the berm, the cavalrymen maintained their
withering gunfire. The tall leader brought his warriors to a
halt and backed them away to a spot just beyond rifle range.
It was clear to the soldiers that the attack was broken, at least
for the moment. They cheered in relief at the little breathing
room they had gained.

Shields turned to check the condition of his men. He
saw three of them holding onto a shoulder or leg as blood

spilled through their fingers. He also saw a horse staggering around, blood streaming down its side.

"Smitty, shoot the horse!" O'Braugh shouted to a corporal as he, too, noticed the wounded animal. "He's liable to go mad and cause the others to stampede."

"Sarge, I can't shoot Dancer. He's been with me for five years," the corporal protested tearfully.

"Shoot him, lad," O'Braugh said more gently. "Can't you see how the poor beast is sufferin'?"

Smitty raised his carbine and fired a bullet into the horse's brain. The horse fell dead. Slowly lowering his rifle, the corporal put his free hand to his eyes.

"Did everyone besides Lieutenant Macklin make it back?" Shields called to his men.

"Zaricore went down," one man responded.

"Wounded or dead?" Shields asked.

"I don't know, Lieutenant. One minute he was ridin' along beside me, the next minute his saddle was empty."

"All right, you men who aren't wounded, help the ones who are. Stop the bleeding. The rest of you, keep alert."

"Want some water, Lieutenant?" O'Braugh asked, handing him a canteen.

"Yes, thank you," Shields said. He lifted the canteen to his lips and took a drink, not realizing until that moment how thirsty he really was. He took several long gulps, then lowered the canteen. "Oh, I'm sorry, Sergeant. I was about to drink it all."

"Drink all you want," O'Braugh said easily. "The one thing we've got plenty of is water. You chose a good spot, with a pump right there."

"Well, that's a good break." Shields drank deeply. "I don't know why I'm so thirsty."

O'Braugh chuckled. "A man's throat always gets dry in battle," he said. He took the canteen back and finished it himself. "Right now, I'd say that gives us a little advantage over Manitoro."

"Manitoro?" Shields interrupted him. "So that was Manitoro?"

O'Braugh nodded and then continued. "We've got water right here. He's got only what he can carry."

"Maybe so, but right now I imagine our men would be glad to change tactical positions with him."

"Tactical positions, maybe," O'Braugh said. "But not commanders. You did a fine job takin' over when Lieutenant Macklin was shot. Even the business of keepin' two men at the rear to provide coverin' fire. Yes, sir, your daddy would be real proud of you," O'Braugh said.

"I assure you, Sergeant," Shields bristled, "I am not doing this for any approval from my father or from anyone who served with him."

"Yes, sir," O'Braugh replied, surprised and stung by Shields's sharp retort. "I'll be seein' to the men." He turned and started to walk away.

"Damn it. Sergeant," Shields called. O'Braugh turned and looked at him. "Sergeant, look, I don't mean to be sharp with you. It's just that, well, for as long as I can remember, my father's been held up to me as someone I should try to emulate."

"Your father was a fine man, Lieutenant. It would be a worthy task for anyone to try and live up to him."

"Perhaps so, but to me he's nothing more than a picture on the mantel. I'd like to be my own man."

O'Braugh's eyes sparkled, and a slow smile spread across his face. "Lad, from what I've seen so far, you've made a fine start. Sure 'n' I'll not be bringin' himself up to you at every turn."

"Thank you," Shields said.

While O'Braugh saw to the positioning of the men and the treatment of the wounded, Shields quietly assessed their situation. Though the Indians outnumbered them by more than three to one, he was reasonably certain they would not try to overrun the soldiers' position. He had established a good defensive position.

As the afternoon wore on, events proved him right. The Indians did not try a frontal attack, though they did fire several long-range, ineffective shots at the soldiers. Eventually they even stopped that, no doubt realizing they were just wasting their bullets. Shields and his men stayed in position as the sun settled lower in the west. The purple clouds were underlined with gold, but the dominant color was the flame of red that spread across the horizon.

"Would you be believin' in portents, sir?" O'Braugh asked Shields as he sat next to him looking at the evening sky.

"Portents?" Shields asked, puzzled.

"Yes, sir. You know, signs, foretellin' the future?"

"No, I can't say that I do. Why? Do you?"

"Well, I'm not believin' in them, mind, but neither do I like to see them flaunted so."

"What portent are you talking about?" Shields asked.

Sergeant O'Braugh pointed toward the western horizon at the smear of red following the sun down. "That, sir," he said. "'Tis for all the world like a smear of blood."

"It's only the refraction of the light waves as the sun sinks lower in the atmosphere," Shields said.

O'Braugh chuckled. "Is that somethin' you learned in your fancy schoolin' back East, sir?"

"Yes," Shields said with a laugh. "I must confess, Sergeant, when I studied that I never thought I'd have an occasion to actually use it. But if it keeps my sergeant from being concerned about portents, then I'm glad to set your mind at ease."

"Aye, and it is at ease," O'Braugh said as he stretched his long legs out and leaned comfortably against a rock to enjoy the quiet evening. The two men silently watched the sun set until darkness settled over them. With the darkness, however, the ease of those few moments was lost, and Shields grew tense.

"Sergeant, I've heard that Indians never attack at night," he said, breaking the silence. "Would that be true?"

"They don't like to fight at night, true enough," O'Braugh explained. "You see, the Apache believes if he gets killed at night, his spirit will only know night in the hereafter. But these fellas . . . well, sir, they're rogues," O'Braugh said. "Even among their own people. I got a feelin' that if they thought they could get away with it, they'd just as soon fight at night as in the daytime."

"What you're saying is there's a possibility they could attack us tonight?" Shields was chilled at the thought.

"Yes, sir."

"All right, I'll keep a double watch," Shields said. "That way if they try any—" A bloodcurdling scream stopped him instantly. It was a long, high-pitched cry, ending with the words, "Help me! Help me!"

"Good Lord, who is that?" Shields asked, unnerved.

"It has to be Zaricore," O'Braugh whispered hoarsely.

"He's the only one didn't make it back, except for Lieutenant Macklin, and I know he was dead."

"Zaricore," one of the men breathed, and the name was repeated on a half dozen lips as it spread through the little group of soldiers.

The scream pierced the darkness again.

"I can't stand it!" someone cried, suddenly. "I'm goin' out there! I'm goin' to get him!" A shadowy figure leapt to its feet.

"Stop that man!" Shields shouted. Two men grabbed the soldier who had started to climb over the berm. Shields hurried over to him. "Get hold of yourself," he ordered sharply.

"My God, sir, listen to him!" the man moaned.

"Do you want it to be you?" Shields asked sternly.

They heard the scream again. Once more it ended with a plea for help.

"Oh, God, why don't they stop?" the soldier pleaded.

"He'll be all right, sir," one of his friends promised Shields. "I won't let him go out there."

"I'm counting on you, trooper," the lieutenant said.

"Lieutenant," one of the other soldiers called out. "We've got to get these men back to the hospital. Two of 'em still got bullets inside."

"Sergeant." Shields signaled to O'Braugh to step away from the men so they could talk. The two men walked to the south end of the berm, apart from the others, talking in low voices.

"Is there any chance the fort will send out a detail looking for us tomorrow?" he asked softly.

"Probably not tomorrow," O'Braugh whispered in reply. "It's not that unusual for a patrol to stay out two or three days. It'll more likely be two days before anyone comes after us."

"Our wounded won't last two more days," Shields said, shaking his head.

"No, sir," O'Braugh agreed.

"Someone is going to have to slip out of here and go to the fort for help," Shields said.

"Yes, sir, I was thinkin' that same thing."

"You take charge of things here."

"Lieutenant, you don't know the country well enough,"

O'Braugh protested. "You'd either be caught by the Indians or wander around all night tryin' to find your way. Besides, you're in command here. You need to stay with the men."

"Perhaps you're right," Shields agreed at last. He was silent for a long moment. "All right, you know these men. Whom should we send?"

"Me."

"You? No, you need to stay here."

"Lieutenant, you're doin' a fine job, sir," O'Braugh said. "You don't need me around here. And I know the land better'n anyone. If I leave now, I can have a whole troop here by noon tomorrow."

They heard the long, bloodcurdling scream again.

"All right," Shields said decisively. "Do it." O'Braugh turned to leave. "And Sergeant?"

"Yes, sir?" O'Braugh looked back at him.

"Be careful. I might want to hear about my father from someone who actually knew him," Shields said softly.

O'Braugh grinned broadly. "Sure an' 'twould be a pleasure to tell you all I know about the great man," he said warmly.

Shields and the others watched as O'Braugh prepared for the journey to the fort. He took off everything that jingled and rattled, emptied his pockets, then ripped up an army blanket and tied it around the hooves of his horse.

"I'll walk him out like this," he explained to them. "When we're far enough away, I'll take the pads off and ride like the fires of Hell are behind me." He handed his carbine to one of the soldiers, his pistol to another. "Keep up with these," he said.

"Sergeant, are you taking no weapons at all?" Shields asked, surprised that he would ride unarmed in hostile country.

"No, sir. They'll just be for slowin' me down, an' they'd be no good anyway. I couldn't be fightin' off the whole band all by myself. The only chance I got is by avoidin' 'em. Besides which, if I get caught, I don't plan on givin' the heathen my guns."

Shields would not have thought of doing it, but he appreciated how shrewd O'Braugh was. "Very well," he said. "Good luck."

Shields walked to the edge of the berm with O'Braugh and watched as he led the horse out into the night. It was so dark that the sergeant had completely disappeared after just a few steps. A few steps beyond that, he could not even be heard. It was as if the sergeant had stepped off the end of the earth.

A few moments later they heard the bloodcurdling scream again, and for an instant Shields froze as he thought it might be his sergeant. But then he realized that it was the same yell they had been hearing all night. And now something about the scream began to nag at him.

"Smitty!" he called to the corporal.

"Yes, sir," Smitty answered.

"Was Zaricore a friend of yours?"

"Yes, sir, a close friend."

"I want you to listen carefully to this voice the next time we hear it. Tell me if you think it's really him."

"Lieutenant?"

"Yes."

"I already been listenin' to it, sir. It's got to be him 'cause there ain't no one else out there. But I have to admit that it don't sound like him. It don't sound *nothin'* like him at all."

"Then who is the poor bastard?" someone asked.

"No one," Shields answered.

"No one? What do you mean, no one, sir? Can't you hear him?"

"Yes, I hear him. That's why I know it isn't anyone really being tortured. Listen to it. It is exactly the same every time. If it really was someone being tortured, don't you think he'd be getting weaker by now?"

The voice screamed, ending again with the plaintive plea, "Help me! Help me!" It sounded exactly as it had every other time.

"The lieutenant's right," one of the soldiers blurted. "That son of a bitch ain't bein' tortured. That's one of the Indians, mocking us, tryin' to make us go crazy."

"He damn near done it," said the soldier who had started over the berm earlier.

"You're all right now, aren't you?" Shields asked him gently. "You don't think that's really anyone being tortured, do you?"

"No, sir, I guess not," the soldier said.

They heard the scream again, and Smitty shouted to

them, "Go ahead! Pluck his eyes out! We don't care!" His shout was followed by the nervous laughter of the other soldiers.

The first pink fingers of dawn touched the cacti. The light was soft. The air was cool. The morning star made a bright pinpoint of light over the purple Mazatzal Mountains, lying in a ragged line to the west. Shields pulled his blanket around him, surprised at how cold it could get at night when it was so hot during the day.

A rustle of wind through feathers caused him to look up just in time to see a golden eagle diving on its prey. The eagle swooped back into the air carrying a tiny desert mouse that kicked fearfully in the eagle's claws. A Gila monster scurried beneath a nearby mesquite tree which was dying of parasitic mistletoe.

Shields took a drink of water and thought of the events of the last twenty-four hours. This time yesterday morning he had been a gentleman officer, a whist partner, and a traveling companion on a luxurious cross-country train trip. He had been a ballroom dandy in his new uniform, and his sketches had entertained the Solingers and other wealthy passengers. Military command was something he had studied, but it was not something he had experienced. Abruptly, in the first hours of his first assignment, he had been thrust into the command of men in combat. He had put his life on the line . . . he had seen men killed. In all likelihood he had killed, for he had seen an Indian go down following one of his shots.

Where are the guidons now? he wondered. *Where are the bands, the parades, the military balls, the teas and receptions, the colonels' ladies and the generals' daughters?* He looked at his men in the gray early-morning light. The three wounded soldiers were lying in the middle of the cantonment, their bandages stained with blood. The others were at their positions around the berm, their eyes tired and red, and their faces haggard from lack of sleep. Though he had authorized a watch of one on and one off during the night, to allow the men to get some rest, he knew none of them had slept. He could not blame them. He had not slept a wink either.

He thought of Sergeant O'Braugh and wondered if he had made it. Somehow, without knowing how he knew, he was positive that the sergeant had made it, and he was confident that a relief column would arrive by noon.

"Lieutenant," one of his men called. "Look." The soldier pointed to a nearby ridge.

Shields saw a long line of Indians, many more than he had seen the day before, and he felt a sense of alarm. With a party that large, the Indians would feel emboldened to attack, and their attack would be successful. He raised his binoculars and was startled to see that the Indians were not being led by the dark-haired warrior of the day before, but by a young woman. He watched in surprise as a young Indian rode down the ridge alone toward the ranch, carrying a white flag.

"Smitty," he called.

"Yes, sir."

"I'm going out to see what they want. If anything happens to me, try to hold them off until noon. I'm sure Sergeant O'Braugh will be back with support by then."

"Yes, sir," Smitty said. With O'Braugh gone, Smitty, a corporal, was the next in command.

Shields mounted his horse and rode out to meet the woman with the white flag. When he reached the rider and saw her blond hair, blue eyes, and fair complexion, he was astounded. "You're a white woman!" he gasped.

"Yes," she said, a slow smile spreading across her lovely face.

"Are you a captive?" Shields blurted.

The woman laughed. It was a rich, tinkling sound, like the rustle of wind chimes. "No. I am Sasha Quiet Stream. Chief Chatoma is my father, or, I should say, my stepfather."

Shields twisted in his saddle and looked at the Indians who lined the ridge behind her. He pointed to them. "Were you with your stepfather when he burned the ranch and massacred the people there? Were you with him when he attacked us last night?" he demanded angrily.

"My father is at peace with the white man. We," she said evenly as she waved an outstretched arm to encompass all the warriors behind her, "are at peace with the white man. We did not kill the ones at the ranch, and we did not attack you last night. It was Manitoro who did these things."

Shields was stunned by her words. "Yes," he said slowly. "Manitoro." He had ridden here prepared for anything but this, and he was silent as he tried to absorb the news.

"You must be new," she said gently.

"Yes," he answered her simply.

"I thought so," Sasha said, smiling broadly. "I have not seen you at the fort before."

"You have been in the fort?" he asked, shocked.

"Yes, many times. My father is ill, and Dr. Hartfield gives him medicine."

Shields rubbed his hand across his chin, feeling the stubble of an overnight's growth of beard. He felt self-conscious that he looked so slovenly, and for a moment he did not know why. Then he realized that, adopted Indian or not, he was responding to her as a very beautiful woman.

"I know Dr. Hartfield," Shields said defensively. "He has never spoken of you." He did not mention that he had spent only five minutes with the doctor.

Sasha smiled knowingly and chose not to comment. Instead she turned her horse to leave. "We go now," she said. "Manitoro is gone. You and your men can ride back to the fort. You will not be harmed. Talk to your soldiers about Sasha Quiet Stream. They will tell you who I am."

Shields sat numbly in his saddle and watched as the young blond woman urged her horse up the hill to join the Indians. Once she reached them, he could see her head nodding as she spoke a few words to them. A couple of them glanced down at Shields, and loud peals of laughter carried to him. A moment later the Indians galloped away, led by Sasha, who rode as effortlessly and gracefully as the wind.

Shields rode back to his men.

"I seen through your spyglasses that you was talkin' to Miss Sasha," Smitty said. "Manitoro's gone, ain't he, sir?"

"You know her?"

"Sure. We all do. She's 'bout the prettiest thing in these parts."

"She's a white woman, riding with the Indians," Shields said, still struggling to put the bizarre situation into perspective.

"She don't just ride with 'em, she's one of 'em," Smitty said. "But she's one of the good ones. If she's here, Manitoro ain't."

"That's something I can count on?" Shields asked.

"Yes, sir." Smitty pointed to the three wounded men. "By the way, sir, I had the men make travois for the wounded. I hope you don't mind."

"Travois?"

"It's like an Indian wagon without wheels," Smitty said, pointing to one of the contraptions already hooked behind a horse.

"Good for you," Shields said. "All right, Corporal, get the men mounted. We're starting back."

They had ridden less than a mile when they met a large relief column from the fort. O'Braugh had brought back an entire troop, commanded by a lieutenant that Shields had not yet met.

"Lieutenant Culpepper, Shields," the lieutenant said. "Didn't have the chance to meet you yesterday." He turned in his saddle. "Bring that ambulance up. Get these wounded inside!" he shouted.

Shields smiled in relief. "Believe me, Lieutenant, this is as good a time as any."

Shields fell in alongside Sergeant O'Braugh. "You made good time, Sergeant," he said.

"Yes, sir. I didn't stop along the way. How are the wounded?" he asked, and he turned to watch as they were loaded into the ambulance.

"I think they'll be all right if we can get the bullets out before they start to fester," Shields said.

"I heard one of the men mention Sasha Quiet Stream," O'Braugh said.

"You know her?" Shields probed.

"Yes, sir. Ever'one out here knows about her."

"Everyone but me, it seems. How did a white girl wind up with the Indians?"

"She was raised by 'em," O'Braugh replied. "Her real name is Lily Mason. Her folks and everyone on her wagon train were killed by Apache. She was the only one left alive."

"And she lives with the very people who killed her parents?" Shields was incredulous.

"Oh, it wasn't Chatoma," O'Braugh said. "He was the one who found her and raised her—treated her like his own daughter. Done a fine job of it, too. I've known lots of women in my day, sir, but none better than Sasha Quiet Stream."

"Now that everyone knows her story, why has nothing been done to reunite her with her people?"

"I told you, sir. All her people are dead."

"Surely she has aunts, uncles, cousins, someone?"

"Could be," O'Braugh agreed. "But if so, they don't even know her . . . probably wouldn't want anything to do with her. No, sir, she's a lot better off right where she is."

Shields did not say anything more, but he found the idea of a white woman being raised by Indians, be they hostile or friendly, very disturbing.

Chapter Four

"**R**aise the right side up a little, Mrs. Kelly," Amy Hartfield said. Two weeks had passed since the arrival of Lieutenant Mark Shields, and now the women of Fort Verde were preparing for the arrival of his fiancée. Susan Hamilton's coach was due in later that day, and Amy was directing some of the wives as they decorated the sutler's store for the dance honoring her. "There, that looks nice, don't you think so, Mr. Branson?"

Farley Branson glanced up from his ledger book to look at the bunting the ladies of the fort were hanging. He was a very important man at Fort Verde, and the store he was commissioned by the army to run served many purposes for the people in this distant outpost. The sutler's store not only provided soldiers with a place to buy necessary items, but also served as a saloon and social hall. In many ways the sutler was the most important man on the post. Getting the appointment to operate one was quite a plum, and Branson had pulled every string he knew to get the commission.

It was a very profitable operation, and Branson was shrewd enough to be generous with such things as decorations and supplies for parties. He furnished, free of cost, the bunting to decorate the hall. He would also provide the canned fruit juices for the punch that would be served. Without a doubt the punch would be spiked, and though he did not provide the liquor free, he was very generous with his credit policy. The liquor that did find its way into the punch would be liquor that was, as yet, unpaid for.

49

The man who had run up the highest debt for liquor was the post commander, Captain Ross. As Branson examined his ledger book, he saw that the amount of money Ross owed him was far out of proportion to the captain's pay. Ross entered the store just as Branson was totaling all his figures.

"Good afternoon, Captain Ross," Branson said.

Ross nodded and then looked over at the women. "They seem to be caught up in the spirit of things," Ross said to Branson.

"Yes, sir, they do at that," Branson agreed. "But then, you know how the ladies are when you mention the possibility of a party. They truly love to socialize and have a good time. There's little enough opportunity for it out here."

"All the more reason I think the War Department should make a regulation prohibiting women from the western frontier."

"You don't mean that, Captain. It would be a bleak place out here without the fairer sex." Without being told, Branson slipped a bottle of whiskey into a cloth bag and surreptitiously handed it to the captain.

"Thank you," Captain Ross said. He cleared his throat. "Uh . . . just mark it in the ledger there if you will."

"I'd be glad to, Captain," Branson said, making the appropriate entry. "By the way, not that I'm worried or anything, but your liquor debt is growing quite large."

"Yes, well, uh, I'll pay you something on it next payday," Captain Ross said.

"No hurry," Branson said, with a wave of his arm. "I'm sure you'll find some way to take care of it."

"Uh, yes, I'm sure," Ross said, coughing nervously and clutching the bag that Branson handed him. Ross was no fool. He knew that Branson was not giving him the whiskey; and he knew that some day there would be a reckoning. It was not good for the commander of a fort to be beholden to a civilian whose business interests were as far-flung as Branson's. Branson had told him that he was investing in land. "As a token of my faith in the future of Arizona, and in the United States Army to make that future bright," Branson once told Ross.

"Where is the young lieutenant?" Branson asked.

"He has taken a scouting party out to look for Manitoro," Captain Ross said. "As you know, there have been a few more attacks since the one on the Webbs a couple of weeks ago."

"I fear Miss Hamilton will be disappointed by his absence when she arrives."

"I'm running an army post, Mr. Branson, not a social club." Ross bristled. His answer was sharper than necessary, brought on in part by his feeling of guilt for allowing himself to get so deeply indebted to Branson.

"Oh, to be sure, to be sure," Branson said. "And as Miss Hamilton is a general's daughter, I'm certain she will understand. You'll get no argument from me, Captain Ross. If you recall, I, for one, have been telling you that you should be even more cautious of the local Indians. I can't believe all of our troubles are caused by one renegade and his followers. I think we are being too complacent with Chatoma."

"Chatoma?" Ross asked, surprised. "Surely you don't suspect him?"

"Why not?"

"What would Chatoma gain by causing difficulty for us?"

"The same thing all the heathens would gain," Branson argued pointedly. "They want white families to think twice before settling this territory out here. It leaves more open space for them."

"I can't believe that of Chatoma. He's been a friend of the whites for as long as I've been out here," Ross protested.

"I will admit that he's a little more devious than Manitoro. The fact that he has raised a white girl as his own, has learned some of the white ways from her, proves that. But in my book it just makes him more dangerous. At least Manitoro is honest in his actions. Everyone knows he hates the white man; everyone knows where he stands. But Chatoma just smiles and speaks soft words. No, sir, it wouldn't surprise me if some of the raids we blame on Manitoro were actually the work of Chatoma."

Ross thoughtfully ran his hand across his chin. "Look here, Branson. Being a civilian, you must sometimes hear things that we in the military don't. Have you heard anything to support what you say?"

Branson's eyes narrowed. "Not exactly," he admitted. "At least, not that I can quote, chapter and verse. But, like you say, I do hear things that the army doesn't, so I keep my ears open."

"You do that, Branson, and if you hear anything that I should know, anything at all, let me know."

"You can count on it, Captain. After all, I have a special interest in seeing that this territory is kept peaceful."

"We all do," Ross said. "I'll see you at the party tonight." He started through the front door but was stopped by Mrs. Hartfield.

"Captain, you will see to it that the uniform is mess dress tonight?" she said, smiling brightly at him.

"I had the first sergeant draw up the order this morning, Mrs. Hartfield," Ross said.

"Good, good. I think a party is much more elegant when the officers and men are properly dressed. And I know Miss Hamilton will expect it."

"When is she supposed to arrive?" Ross asked.

"Emily Rourke is meeting the train in Prescott right now."

Susan Hamilton stepped off the train wearing a brown wool traveling suit with hooded cape, polonaise, and round skirt. In her hand she clutched a smart leather purse, and on her head she wore a bonnet, gaily decorated with green and yellow silk flowers. If Emily had not been given a description of the young woman she was to pick up, she would have known nevertheless that this was her charge.

Emily had been sitting on the seat of the coach waiting for the train, and when she saw the young woman step onto the platform, she said quietly to herself, "Now that's what a real lady looks like—not somebody dressed in cotton and buckskin like me. And have you ever seen such a beautiful hat?"

Emily did not yearn for such clothes. Even if she had them, she would not be able to wear them out here. They were totally impractical, even among women who did not have jobs as physically demanding as hers. Yet she could recall a time when she was younger, back East in the days when she was being courted by Sergeant Rourke, when all the ladies wore such elegant clothes. Even though she had worked as a nanny, she had been able to wear nice things, and seeing them now kindled memories of those days and reminded her of her courting. When she thought of Susan

Hamilton going through the same thing with the new lieutenant, she felt a warm spot in her heart.

Kevin O'Braugh had told her that the new lieutenant had been coming around quite nicely. He had acquitted himself well in the engagement at the ranch house, and the enormous chip he had seemed to wear on his shoulder was gone. O'Braugh said the boy was of good stock, and events seemed to be proving him right. Emily hoped the young woman was good enough for him. She climbed down from the seat and walked up the depot platform toward the young woman.

"You'd be Miss Hamilton?"

The woman had been looking in the opposite direction, and she turned when Emily spoke. A flash of dark hair showed under her bonnet. Her complexion was smooth, her features well formed, and her eyes a beautiful shade of blue. Yet there was a hardness in her eyes, a flinty edge that startled Emily.

"Yes," she said. "Where is Mark?"

"Lieutenant Shields is back at the fort," Emily said. "I've come to get you."

"You? And how, pray tell, are you to fetch me?"

"I've a stagecoach over there," Emily said, pointing to her coach.

Susan looked toward it, then screwed her face up in a frown. "Where's the driver?"

"Why, I'm the driver," Emily explained.

"You? I've never heard of such a thing. A woman driving a stagecoach," Susan snapped.

Emily chuckled. "Yes, well, I imagine you'll see more than one new thing out here. Has your luggage been taken from the train? I'll see that it's put on the coach."

"Oh. Are you a drayman as well?" Susan asked.

"When necessary," Emily answered. Though she was trying to be friendly, the young woman's sharp tongue was making it difficult.

Emily had never seen so much luggage accompany one person. There were two trunks and four suitcases, plus assorted boxes and packages. It took two of the railroad men several minutes to load the stage, filling the luggage boot and as a last resort, putting some on top. Susan stood by, sharply critical of the least bump. Finally everything was loaded and they were ready to depart.

"Mark should've come," Susan said petulantly. "I can't understand why he didn't."

"I'm sure he would have been here if he could," Emily explained.

"I know of nothing that is more important than meeting his fiancée."

"But surely, being the daughter of a general, you can understand the importance of a young officer performing his duty as assigned."

"Duty? In this godforsaken land?" Susan screwed up her lips distastefully.

"Yes, well, it does grow on you. We're ready to go. Would you like to ride up top with me?"

"Heavens, no! What would make you ask such a thing?"

"Well," Emily said, "it is considered to be a privilege."

"Thank you, but that is one privilege I shall gladly forgo."

"Whatever you like," Emily said. She could have reminded the young woman that the top seat was more comfortable than the seats inside. More importantly, the top seat was above the plume of dirt and dust kicked up by the wheels. If Susan rode with her, she would arrive at the fort nearly as fresh as she had been when she stepped off the train. By riding inside the coach, she would be subjected to the swirling cloud of dirt and would arrive terribly soiled. But Susan's attitude had been such that Emily was just as glad the woman turned her down. She could do without her company.

They had been under way for the better part of the morning. Susan had changed seats from side to side and corner to corner, trying to find the most comfortable position. She felt as if she were dangling from the end of a string, bouncing this way and that as the coach lurched first one way and then another. Adding to the unpleasantness of the rough ride were the dirt and dust that swirled in. She could see it in the folds of her beautiful new dress, feel it in her eyes and on her skin, and taste it in her mouth. She looked down at the dress, recalling her dreams of the first moment she would meet Shields out here in the West. He would be wearing a dress uniform, complete with cape and saber, and she would be in the brown traveling suit. He would sweep her away to an elegant landaulet, pulled by a team of matching snow-white horses, driven by a liveried driver.

In her more practical moments, she realized that some of her dream was probably idealized. But never in her wildest nightmare had she expected to be thrust into the back of a stagecoach with a woman driver for half a day's journey across the most desolate country in the world before she even had the chance to see her fiancé. It simply was not fair, and she intended to write her father about it as soon as she arrived.

Suddenly the coach stopped, and Susan looked through the window to see why. What she saw made her heart leap to her throat in fear. There, no more than fifty yards away from the coach, she saw a line of Indians on horseback, at least twenty of them! She whimpered in alarm, closed the leather curtains on the coach, and then shrank back in terror. All sorts of thoughts raced through her head, stories she had read of bloody massacres, visions of her brunette hair decorating the inside of some warrior's tepee.

Susan heard the woman driver speaking to the Indians. *My God! She is speaking to them in their own language!* The language had a guttural, clicking, unpleasant sound to it, like the fluttering wings of blackbirds, and she felt a chill just listening to them speak. Then the language turned to English, and she could understand what was being said.

"It warms my heart to see my young friend. You brighten my day," Emily said.

"My journey has been made lighter because we have met," another woman's voice replied.

There was something strange about the words. Susan thought about it for a moment and then realized that they were spoken virtually without accent! How could an Indian woman speak English so flawlessly?

Susan peeked through the crack in the leather curtains and saw that the woman was not Indian. It was a white woman, a young blonde no older than Susan, dressed as an Indian and riding as one of them.

"How may I show my friendship?" Emily asked.

"Have you any tobacco?" the blonde replied. "My father wishes some. I can pay you."

"Your money is no good with me, Sasha," Emily said. "I have some tobacco, and your father is welcome to it. Tell him it is from a friend."

"Thank you," Sasha answered. "It will please him. May we live till we meet again."

Susan watched as the blond woman rode back to rejoin the Indians, and then she watched them ride away. She was confused. The woman was definitely white and spoke English without an accent, yet the words and phrases she used were unusual. "My journey is lighter because we have met," and "May we live till we meet again." Who was this person, and why was she riding with the Indians?

The door suddenly flew open, and Susan gasped in fear. It was only the driver.

"Are you all right?" Emily asked.

"Yes, yes, I'm fine. What was all that about?"

"The girl just wanted some tobacco for her father, that's all. She's Chief Chatoma's daughter. He's a good man, a friend to the whites, and I'm glad to help him out anytime I can."

"But that was a white girl."

"Yes," Emily said without elaborating. "I guess she was at that. Well, sit back and get comfortable, Miss Hamilton. We'll be at the fort in little more than an hour."

When the coach arrived at the fort, half a dozen women were waiting under the porch of the headquarters building. A banner that read "Welcome Susan Hamilton!" was stretched across the front. One of the women stepped over to the coach and opened the door, smiling broadly.

"Hello, dear. I'm Mrs. Amy Hartfield. On behalf of the ladies, officers, and men of Fort Verde, we welcome you. This is Mrs. Dora McCorkle, Mrs. Julie Bates, Mrs. Lucinda Keogh, Mrs. Martha Seabaugh, and Mrs. Sarah Turner." As Amy called each name a woman stepped forward and curtsied.

Susan stepped down and looked around. The buildings were gray and weather-beaten, the ground hard-packed clay. The vegetation, what little there was, was dry and brown. A dust devil gathered itself on the parade ground and whirled its way across the post, finally beating itself against a low, ugly building on the far side.

"Oh, what a lovely dress!" Mrs. McCorkle exclaimed.

Susan looked at the woman. How could she be so mean? How could she be so cruel and insensitive to mention her dress now, as filthy as it was? Tears welled in her eyes, and she blinked several times to keep from wailing out loud. She would run away and cry now, if she only knew where to go.

"We have a little tea arranged," one of the others said quickly. "I hope you'll do us the honor of attending."

"No!" Susan said sharply. Then, softening it a little, she added, "Thank you, I'd rather not."

"I . . . I imagine you must be terribly worn out from your trip," Amy offered. "Come along. You'll be staying with Dr. Hartfield and me for the time being."

"Thank you," Susan managed to say.

"But, Mrs. Hartfield, the tea," one of the other ladies put in.

"Let me see to Miss Hamilton, and I'll come back and join you," Amy said. She smiled. "We can have the tea in her honor, even if she isn't there."

Susan had already walked away from the others. Amy joined her quickly and then led the way to her house. Amy's house looked quite large from outside, but as they drew closer, Susan saw that was because the house was attached to the post hospital.

"There's a lovely room upstairs," Amy said. "This house was designed for a married surgeon with children." Amy got a faraway look in her eyes. "James and I—that's the doctor—we never had any children." She laughed, as if she could dismiss twenty years of heartache in one gasp. "James says the soldiers are our children, and sometimes I think he's right. Some of them are barely more than boys. They come out here, away from home for the first time, lonely, homesick, sometimes frightened. In a lonely post like this, we all become quite attached to each other, though I'm sure you will soon learn that."

"I don't intend to stay here long enough to learn anything," Susan said. "As soon as Mark and I are married, I shall wire my father and have him obtain new orders for Mark. He wasn't meant to waste his life here in this . . . this barren wasteland."

"Why, my dear, this is where the army is needed most. James wouldn't think of serving anywhere else."

"Which one of those ladies was the commanding officer's wife?" Susan demanded.

"Oh, none of them," Amy answered sweetly. "I'm the only officer's wife on the post."

"What? You mean there are no other officers' wives? But how can you exist that way?"

"Several of the NCOs are married," Amy explained. "They are wonderful ladies, and we get along splendidly."

"NCO wives. That explains how that woman could be so cruel as to deliberately insult me about my dress."

"Why, whatever do you mean? She paid you a compliment, and she was right. It is a lovely dress."

"It's filthy from that horrid stagecoach ride out here," Susan complained. "I . . . I have a terrible headache. If you don't mind, I would like to go to my room and lie down with a damp cloth on my forehead."

"Yes, of course," Amy said, crestfallen by Susan's attitude. "It's right up here."

At the very moment Susan was climbing the stairs to lie down, Mark Shields was no more than ten miles from the fort. Fourteen men were with him: twelve privates, one corporal, and one sergeant. The sergeant was a veteran of several years' campaign service, his hair salt-and-pepper gray, his face lined and weathered. He was chewing tobacco. He leaned over to expectorate and then wiped the back of his hand across his chin.

"Lieutenant, whyn't you take a look-see on that ridge yonder with them fancy spyglasses of yours," the sergeant suggested.

"Did you see something?" Shields asked.

"Well, no, sir," the sergeant admitted. "But when you been around as long as I been, you don't see Injuns, you just sort'a feel them. And I been feelin' 'em now for the better part of an hour."

"Sergeant, if you say you feel them, that's good enough for me," Shields said. "Maybe we'd better—"

The singing swoosh of an arrow cut him off. It made a hollow *thock* as it hit Shields's saddle. The arrow stuck, and the shaft quivered right in front of his leg. Shields, struck dumb for just an instant by the shock of the near miss, looked at it in surprise. His horse jumped once, nervously, though it had not been hit.

"There they are!" the veteran shouted. He pointed to the hill that he had asked Shields to check out. A band of Apache came swooping over the top, whooping and shouting at the top of their lungs. Shields did not take time to count them, but he estimated that there were about thirty braves in the band.

"Let's get out of here!" Shields shouted, and he slapped his heels against the flanks of his horse, urging it on. They raced along the bank of Beaver Creek, occasionally slipping down into the water itself and sending up sheets of spray.

Shields led the men out of the creek bed and onto flat terrain to an area large enough to allow him to swing his men around. At first it was unclear to the others what he was doing; then they realized that their lieutenant had, by describing a large circle, turned the retreat into an attack. The Indians realized it at about the same time. They wheeled about in confusion and started to retreat.

"Let's go get them!" Shields shouted. He charged after the confused, retreating Indians, urging his horse on, faster and faster. Rapidly, he drew closer to the Indians, though he was pulling away from his own men. Within a short time he was abreast with the rear ranks of the Indians.

The Indians had abandoned all thought of attack and were now fleeing for their lives. They turned their rifles toward Shields and fired. He heard the angry buzz of half a dozen bullets go by him. He pulled his pistol, took slow and deliberate aim, and watched as his target tumbled from the saddle. The Indians broke up, scattering in every direction like a covey of flushed quail. It was now no longer possible to pursue them as a body, so Shields broke off the charge, regrouped his men, and started them back toward the fort.

"Lieutenant, that was pretty slick, turnin' us around like that so's we was on the attack. Where'd you learn that?" the sergeant asked.

"It was one of Wellington's tactics, used against Napoleon's cavalry at Waterloo."

"You knew this fella Wellington, did you?"

"You might say that," Shields said, smiling. "At least I read his book."

"Well, if he wrote a book, he must've been a smart man. But I don't reckon he was any smarter'n you. Writin' it in a book is one thing; doin' it is somethin' else again," the sergeant said, his voice showing his admiration for his lieutenant.

* * *

Late that afternoon, freshened up somewhat and dressed in a clean gown, Susan came downstairs. She stood under the sally port and watched as the fort was turned out for retreat ceremony. This, at least, was familiar to her. She stood there as the bugler played retreat and the flag was lowered. It was a ceremony she had witnessed many times, growing up as she had in a military family. If only she could find a few other comforting things about this place.

The commanding officer came over to speak with her after the ceremony. Susan was surprised to see that he was only a captain. Why, he was as old as her father, and her father was a general!

"Miss Hamilton, I am Captain Alan Ross. As commanding officer, let me welcome you to Fort Verde."

"Thank you, Captain Ross."

"I've had the honor of serving with your father. When you write him, you must extend my regards."

"I will, of course."

"Corporal of the guard! Patrol returning!" someone shouted.

"Well, Miss Hamilton," Captain Ross said. "That'll be your Lieutenant Shields."

For the first time since stepping off the train Susan felt a sense of elation. Here, at last, was the reason she had traveled across three quarters of a continent. She was about to see the man she would marry.

Susan remembered the evening he had proposed marriage to her. She could recall the smell of the spring flowers along the trail at the academy that overlooked the beautiful Hudson River. How handsome Shields had been then, in his cadet gray. How lovely had been the setting. And now, she was about to see him again.

The riders came through the gates of the post, rode to the center of the parade ground, and stopped. Shields was at the head of the group. She saw him ride out from the others and then give the orders dismissing them. He dismounted, and one of the other soldiers took his horse. Captain Ross walked out toward him, and she could hear his voice as he gave his report.

"We engaged the Indians in midafternoon, Captain," she heard him say. "We killed one, but the rest got away."

"Did you sustain any casualties?"

"None, sir."

"Very well, you are dismissed."

"Thank you, sir."

Shields saluted and then strode toward Susan with a big smile on his face.

"Sue," he said, reaching for her.

Susan had never seen anyone as filthy as this man who reached for her. He was not the fresh-scrubbed, clean-cheeked, handsome young cadet with whom she had fallen in love. He was a filthy, unshaven, thoroughly disgusting-looking man. He smelled of horse and sweat and other things she could not identify. He looked like the derelicts she sometimes saw in the gutters by the saloons in the seedier parts of Washington. And he was trying to put his arms around her! She recoiled in horror.

At first Shields was surprised, but then he smiled, good-naturedly. "Oh, I'm sorry. I guess I am pretty much of a mess. I forget what this looks like to someone who's seeing it all for the first time. But you'll get used to it. It's part of life out here."

"I'll never get used to life out here!" she said, stamping her foot.

"Well, darling, you're going to have to get used to it," Shields said. "It's to be our home. Speaking of which, come along, let me show you where we'll live. I've been spending all my spare time working on it. I'm quite proud of my handiwork, and I think you will be, too."

They started walking across the quadrangle toward a row of small buildings. It was a walk of fifty or sixty yards, and during that short walk twenty or more enlisted men walked by and saluted. Shields chuckled.

"What is it?" Susan demanded.

"The curiosity of the men," he said. "They are all so eager to get a look at you that they are breaking their necks to get over here and salute me. Normally they would go out of their way to avoid saluting."

"You should put them in their place," she said imperiously.

"Oh, they aren't a bad bunch. Besides, it's different out here on the frontier. Here, we have to depend on each other. There are times when your very life depends on an enlisted man, or his on you. That makes us a little closer than the parade-ground army back East."

"Parade-ground army?"

"Yes. We call them garrison guardians," Shields said with a sense of pride. "You know, troops who polish shoes and brass, and then march in parade every Saturday."

"And you find that distasteful?"

"Well, no. But you must admit that leading a squadron of men in battle is certainly more rewarding than leading them down Pennsylvania Avenue."

"At least the garrison guardians, as you call them, have the opportunity to take a bath," Susan said.

"Yes, well, wait until you see me at the dance tonight. I'll be the clean cadet who captured your heart. And my men? Why, they'll look like cadets on parade."

"Dance? Oh, no, Mark, I don't want to go to a dance out here. How do they decorate? Bunting and cactus flower?" She scowled in distaste. "I can think of nothing more dreary than that."

"Darling, you have no choice," Shields explained. "Bunting and cactus flower or not, the ladies of this post have been working for the entire week to get the sutler's store decorated for you. It would be an unforgivable breach of etiquette for you to refuse."

"The ladies of the post? It is my understanding that only one officer is married. That means there is only one lady of the post. The other women are NCO wives, hardly in our social class," Susan complained haughtily.

"Our social class?" Shields sighed deeply. "Very well, then we'll consider the wishes of the lady of the post. Her husband is, after all, a major."

"All right, if you insist, I'll go. Why are we stopping here?"

"This is it."

"This is what?"

"This is our house. At least, it's going to be."

Susan looked at the little shack. The woodshed behind her father's house was larger. She felt sick, and she bit her lower lip to keep from crying out.

"Wait till you see what I've done inside," Shields said proudly, not noticing her dismay. "I've built shelves and drawers, and a good, sturdy table. Oh, it's a fine place. All it needs is a woman's touch. Mrs. Rourke—you met her, she's the stage driver—said she would pick up some material in town. Mrs. Hartfield said she would help you make curtains. I was going to have it done already, but they said I should let you choose the color. Come on, let me show you inside."

Shields started for the door, but Susan hesitated. "What is it?" he asked. "What's wrong?"

"Nothing," Susan said. "It's just that if we're going to the dance tonight, you'd better start getting cleaned up."

"Oh, yes, I guess you're right," Shields said. He smiled again. "Well, we can look at it tomorrow. You'll have plenty of time. The wedding is scheduled for nine in the morning."

"Tomorrow morning?" Susan was horrified.

"Why, yes. You did come out here to marry me, didn't you? There's no sense in you being a burden on the Hartfields for longer than a day. We even have an Episcopal priest coming over from Prescott, and Bishop Whiteside has granted special permission to waive the posting of banns."

"That's nice," Susan said quietly.

"I thought you'd like it. Well, I'll walk you to the Hartfields'. I have to get cleaned up."

Never had the sutler's store looked more festive than it did that night. Bunting in red, white, and blue was hung from every wall, and streamers of the same colors flowed from the center of the ceiling to each corner. A long table had been drawn to one side of the room, covered with white linen, and set with plates of sandwiches, dried fruits, cookies, and cakes. A large, cut-glass punch bowl, filled with a fruit-juice concoction that had been liberally spiked with several different types of blended whiskey, dominated the center of the table.

The band sat on a raised dais, their instruments gleaming brightly in the reflected glow of candles affixed to the music stands. Additional illumination was provided by kerosene lanterns so that the sutler's store was ablaze with light. Even this contributed to the gaiety, since kerosene and candles were too expensive for general use. The barracks and the NCO homes were generally lighted with rags or other artificial wicks soaked in meat grease. They made a smelly, inadequate, but cheap light.

The officers and men were all wearing their mess-dress uniforms, and the women were dressed in their finest ball gowns. Disdaining the idea of a party out here, Susan had purposely chosen not to wear her best gown. Nevertheless, the women all came to examine her dress and to compliment her on its beauty.

"Thank you for not showing them up," Shields said under his breath, misunderstanding the reason she had dressed down. Clearly, Susan realized, he thought she had left her best ball gown packed so the others would not be embarrassed.

"Oh, there's Sergeant O'Braugh and Mrs. Rourke. But then, you've met Mrs. Rourke, haven't you?" Shields said.

Susan had to look twice. The beautiful, exquisitely dressed woman before her seemed a totally different person from the one who had driven the coach earlier that day.

Emily laughed. "I guess I do look a little different," she said, as if reading Susan's mind. "But I'm like the rest of the ladies around here. I also enjoy getting dressed up occasionally."

"Welcome to Fort Verde, Miss Hamilton," Sergeant Major O'Braugh said. "You've a fine man in the lieutenant. If you don't mind my sayin' so, sir," he added to Shields.

Shields had not spoken a word since O'Braugh had come over to them. He was looking thoughtfully at the Medal of Honor on O'Braugh's tunic. "I didn't know about that," he said, pointing to the medal.

"Aye, the medal. 'Twas himself, your father, who caused me to get that. So it's as much his as 'tis mine."

"Lieutenant, your father was a brave man, sure enough," Emily put in quickly. "But I'll not be lettin' Sergeant O'Braugh put himself down so. He got that medal by running out in the face of a Confederate charge and picking up the colonel, who had fallen mortally wounded. General Sickles witnessed the act of bravery."

"I'm sorry I wasn't able to help your father, lad," O'Braugh said gently. "I would have liked for you to have known him."

"I thank you for trying, Sergeant Major," Shields said.

"Choose your partners for the Virginny reel!" the bandmaster called, and the lines were formed.

As the dance went on into the night, it was obvious that everyone present was enjoying it. Captain Ross was in a corner, nearly insensate from drink but with the excuse that this was a party. Amy danced with her husband, then smiled graciously as the younger soldiers shyly asked her to dance with them. The NCO wives were having a great time as well, not only dancing with their husbands, but entertaining all the men. The sharing of the wives during such dances was not at all suspect, for it was expected of the wives to dance every dance to make the soldiers' plight on the frontier a bit easier. Even Emily danced until her feet hurt, but Susan danced only once with Shields. Then, pleading extreme tiredness from her journey, she spent the rest of the evening sitting in the shadows of the storage room, looking out on the party through tear-dimmed eyes.

"I know exactly what you're thinking, Miss Hamilton. It's a far cry from a military ball in Washington, isn't it?"

Susan turned toward the speaker and saw a tall, handsome man, elegantly dressed in civilian evening clothes.

"I'm Farley Branson, the sutler here. I'm sure you don't remember me, though I did meet you once at a party given by General and Mrs. Dobson," he said, making every effort to be charming.

"Oh. Do you know General Dobson?" Susan asked, her spirits soaring. General Dobson was her father's commander.

"Oh, heavens, yes. Bob and I are old friends. I met him a long time ago, through Secretary Steward."

Well, Susan thought, *here at last is someone who can talk about the Washington social scene on my level.* She warmed to the handsome civilian.

"Let me get something for you to drink," Branson offered. When he saw her frown, he smiled and shook his head. "I don't mean the punch. They seem to be swilling it down all right, but only a drunken Indian could possibly enjoy it. I have a fine claret I think you would appreciate."

"Why, thank you," Susan said. "Thank you very much. That's very kind of you."

"Not at all. The kindness is yours for taking the time to talk with me. You don't know how lonesome it gets out here without someone who shares the same social status—or, at least, the social graces."

"I assure you, Mr. Branson, Lieutenant Shields has all the social graces anyone might want," Susan said, defending her fiancé with more zeal than she really felt, if only to ease her conscience for enjoying the company of this exciting man.

"I'm sure he does," Branson agreed. "Though how long he will keep it is another matter. Service out here brutalizes the most cultured of men."

"It doesn't seem to have affected you," Susan noted.

Branson smiled. "Well, my dear, I'm not exactly a warrior. I'm a businessman. Excuse me, I'll get the claret."

In the far corner of the sutler's store, O'Braugh brought a glass of punch to Emily. As they drank their punch, they looked around at the others. Everyone was having a fine time, it seemed, except for Lieutenant Mark Shields. He was standing over at the bar, brooding over a drink, staring into the shadows of the storage room, where his fiancée sat in animated conversation with the sutler.

"You know, Emily," O'Braugh said, using her first name, though it was something he seldom did in public. He held his glass out in a gesture pointing toward Susan and the sutler. "If you'll be excusin' the language, I'll be tellin' you I never liked that good-for-nothin' son of a bitch anyway."

"Aye," Emily said. "Nor the horse he rode in on."

O'Braugh chuckled, and the two touched their glasses together.

"The young lieutenant's a better man than Miss Hamilton is a woman, Kevin. I'm hopin' she'll go back to where she came from and leave the boy be."

" 'Twould be best for all," O'Braugh agreed.

Chapter Five

The guards at Fort Verde spent the last two hours of their night watch in the exquisite stillness that has been the private dominion of soldiers long before Roman sentries stood the watch with Caesar's legions. Now, smells of brewing coffee and cooking bacon stirred their appetites and told them their long night's vigil was nearly over. A short while earlier, the guards had been surprised to see half a dozen women hurrying through the early-morning darkness, heading for the post chapel. The industrious ladies had gotten up before reveille, rising as early as the cooks. Soon the chapel, like the mess hall, was an island of light in the predawn gloom.

Mrs. McCorkle's rooster, as usual, was the first to announce the dawn. It had already crowed three times before the post bugler came from the orderly room, slipping his suspenders up over his shoulders as he hurried toward the megaphone mounted on a stand in the quadrangle in front of the flagpole. The bugler raised the trumpet to his lips and blew reveille. Almost immediately the barracks began glowing with lamps as the soldiers reemerged into the world they had abandoned the night before.

In the chapel, the women were oblivious to the early-morning calls. Most of the NCO wives were laundresses. By reveille they had usually put in at least a quarter of a day's work. This morning, however, their spirits were much more buoyant than usual. They were having a fine time working together and talking about the wedding that would take place that morning.

"I'm baking pies," Mrs. McCorkle said from the top of a ladder, where she was busily attaching pine boughs to the cornice. Although Amy Hartfield was not with the wives this morning, she had joined Dora McCorkle and the others the day before to gather the pine boughs and flowers to decorate the post chapel.

"When we finish here, me an' Julie and Lucinda will be fryin' chickens," Sarah Turner put in.

"I already fried some chicken for Martin to take with him. He'll be missing the wedding. He's got escort detail," Lucinda told the others. "What are you cookin', Martha?"

"I'm cooking my candied yams," Martha answered.

"Oh, Martha, you'll have to give the new bride your recipe for your yams. They are so good."

"Yes, we should all give her our favorite recipe and a pounding," Julie added excitedly. "I think poundings are such fun, don't you?"

"What is a pounding?" Sarah asked.

"Why, it's where we all bring a pound of something the new bride will need—a pound of flour, a pound of cornmeal, something like that. It's especially fun when you bring a recipe to go along with the ingredients."

"Do you think the new bride is going to like it out here?"

"Of course she will. We have a fine time out here, don't we?"

"Yes, but she isn't like us. She's a general's daughter. Did you see her at the party last night? She didn't seem to enjoy it much."

"Don't hold that against her. Just think back to the time you first came here. What did you think of it?"

"I thought it was heaven," Dora McCorkle said. "John and I had been up in Dakota Territory. Have you ever spent a winter in Dakota Territory?"

Everyone laughed at the last remark as they continued to work busily to make the chapel suitable for the wedding.

A wedding, like the dance the night before, was a social event of great significance. It was like Christmas and Thanksgiving and everyone's birthday rolled into one. Everyone on the post was excited by the prospect, and most work and punishment details had been altered to take the wedding into account.

*   *   *

But there was one group of soldiers who would miss the wedding. That was the group that had been selected to escort the coach back to Prescott. Emily had spent the night at the post as a guest of Dora McCorkle, and she would be returning to Prescott this morning, escorted by a detail provided by the fort. Six volunteers, led by Lucinda's husband, Sergeant Martin Keogh, made up the escort. As directed, they gathered at the front gate right after breakfast. O'Braugh came out, ostensibly to inspect the escort detail, but in reality to tell Emily good-bye. He had just finished his inspection of the detail when Sergeant Keogh pointed to the coach, rolling across the post toward the gate.

"Here she comes now, Sarge."

O'Braugh walked toward the coach, and Emily hauled back on the ribbons and set the brake.

"I've got your detail mounted and ready to go," O'Braugh called up to her.

"Thank you, Kevin," Emily said. She brushed her hair back from her face and smiled. "And thanks for showin' me such a good time at the dance last night. It's been a long time since I was at a fancy dress ball like that."

"I was glad to," O'Braugh said. "I'm thinkin' 'tis a shame you won't be stayin' 'round for the weddin'. The ladies have been workin' since the middle of the night, gettin' the chapel ready and cooking their favorite concoctions. It should be a fine event, what with the weddin' and the eatin' afterward. I'm lookin' forward to it."

Emily chuckled. "Is it the weddin' you're lookin' forward to, Kevin O'Braugh, or the eatin' that'll come later?"

"One's a part of the other," O'Braugh said, laughing at her challenge.

"You! Sergeant Major! Hold that stage!" a woman's voice called.

O'Braugh and Emily quickly looked around and were stunned when they saw Susan Hamilton hurrying across the post grounds, followed by three soldiers struggling under a load of luggage.

"What is it, Miss Hamilton?" O'Braugh asked.

Susan jerked the door open and climbed into the coach. "What is it?" she demanded. "What does it look like? I'm leaving this godforsaken place. I'm getting out of here. And you," she said to the startled driver of the coach. "See if you can manage to miss a few of the potholes and bumps you showed me on the way out here."

Emily was aghast. She stared at O'Braugh as she climbed down from the driver's box to supervise the loading of the luggage. Susan sat, sulking, inside the coach.

"Did you know about this?" O'Braugh asked Emily quietly.

"No," she replied, under her breath. "Not a thing of it."

O'Braugh walked around to the side of the coach and looked through the window. Susan was dabbing at her eyes with a handkerchief.

"Sure an' it couldn't be as bad as all that, lass," O'Braugh said gently. "Would you be wantin' to talk about it? Maybe we could work things out."

Susan glared at him. "Sergeant Major O'Braugh," she said in a dry, brittle voice. "If I want fatherly solicitations, I can get them from a general. I don't need them from a lowly sergeant. Now, if you would be so kind, please tell that woman teamster that her only passenger is aboard and would appreciate it if she would hurry."

"Yes, miss," O'Braugh said, stung by Susan's sharp retort. He looked over at Emily, but she was finished with the loading and had heard Susan's request that they hurry.

"We're on our way, Miss Hamilton," Emily said coolly. "I hope you have a pleasant trip."

"That hardly seems possible in this contraption," Susan replied haughtily.

Emily shook her head sadly and then put her hand and foot to the wheel to climb aboard. She glanced at O'Braugh. "Perhaps you should find young Mark," she suggested in a soft voice. "He might need a kind word or two."

"Aye," O'Braugh said, winking at her. "I'll go look for him now."

O'Braugh stepped back as Emily, seated on the driver's box, whistled at the team and snapped the whip just over their heads. The horses strained forward in their harness, and the coach rolled through the gate and onto the road. The six men of the cavalry escort split into groups, with two riding in front, two to the rear, and one on each side.

O'Braugh waited until the gates were closed behind the coach. Then he started back across the parade ground in search of Mark Shields. He passed the chapel and heard the women laughing inside, still busily preparing for the ceremony. Evidently no one had told them that the wedding was off, that the bride-to-be was on her way to Prescott. In a way, O'Braugh felt as sorry for the ladies of the post as he did for Shields. In fact, a part of him felt that Shields was much better off without the woman. Of course, it was not his place to make such an observation—at least not aloud, and certainly not to Mark Shields. Nevertheless, he was sorry that the young man would be suffering from heartbreak, for he well knew that heartbreak could occur whether the object of one's love deserved it or not. But, when he considered everything, O'Braugh believed it was all for the better.

O'Braugh searched the entire post, looking first in Lieutenant Shields's quarters and then in the stable, the orderly room, the supply room, even the surgeon's quarters. Finally, when he had just about exhausted every possible place, he thought of the sutler's store. The front of the sutler's store was like a general store, but the back served as a saloon. There all ranks, officers and enlisted men alike, could buy liquor by the drink.

O'Braugh looked into the back room, not really expecting to find the young lieutenant there. To his surprise, however, Shields was sitting alone at a table in the back of the room. A bottle of whiskey sat on the table in front of him, and his hand was wrapped around a glass. O'Braugh took off his cap and walked over to the table.

"Lieutenant, top o' the mornin' to you, sir," he said.

Shields held out his hand. "Have a seat, Sergeant Major," he invited. "Join me. Wang," he called. Branson's Chinese employee stuck his head through the door that led to the kitchen and stockroom. "An extra glass for the sergeant major."

"Yes, I bling, quick-quick," Wang answered.

"Never mind the extra glass," O'Braugh called. "Bring us both coffee."

Wang nodded his head and then shuffled off to fill the order. O'Braugh knew he had nearly overstepped his bounds by ordering coffee for the lieutenant, but Shields did not say anything about it.

"Everything going all right?" Shields asked. "All the work details in place?"

"Aye, Lieutenant, all the men are at their tasks."

Shields took another swallow of whiskey, made a face, and wiped the back of his hand across his mouth as he set the glass back down. "What is it, then?" he asked.

"Beg pardon, sir?"

"What is it? Why did you come look me up? You didn't just happen in here, did you, Sergeant Major?"

"No, sir," O'Braugh said. He cleared his throat. "Lieutenant, I was standin' at the front gate when the stage passed through. I'd just performed the escort detail inspection and thought to bid Mrs. Rourke farewell."

"I hope you extended my best wishes," Shields said. "She's a very nice lady, Mrs. Rourke."

"Aye, sir, one of the best, I'd say," O'Braugh said. "And she's taken with you, lad, that's for sure."

"I'm flattered," Shields replied.

"Lieutenant, I saw Miss Hamilton on the stage."

"Then she made it all right?"

"Aye, sir. You're not surprised?"

"No," Shields said. "Miss Hamilton has seen fit to call off the wedding."

"Oh, I'm sorry, lad."

"It's only temporary, you understand," Shields went on. "She's had second thoughts about living out here in this . . . this remote outpost," he went on.

"'Tis a place that requires fortitude, I'll admit," O'Braugh said.

"Perhaps it's for the best," Shields suggested.

"Aye, sir. Perhaps it is."

"After all, even our commanding officer feels it is inappropriate to bring wives into such a place."

"I've heard him express the sentiment," O'Braugh agreed.

"So, I can't be blaming Miss Hamilton for agreeing with him, can I?"

"I suppose not," O'Braugh said. He had been choosing his words carefully and measuring Shields's mood.

Wang arrived with the coffee, setting the full pot and the two cups on the table.

"Take the whiskey, Wang," O'Braugh ordered, deciding he could take strong action. He corked the bottle and handed it to the waiter.

"Just a minute," Shields said sharply, lifting his hand to

snatch the bottle from Wang, who was beyond the lieutenant's reach. "I'm not through with that bottle."

"Aye, lad, you're through with it," O'Braugh said. "Get it out of here, Wang. Now!" Wang scuffled into the kitchen.

"Sergeant Major, you are stepping over the line," Shields said angrily, warning him.

"Lieutenant, you can court-martial me if you've a mind to, sir," he said. "But I'll not sit idly by and watch you destroy yourself with whiskey. 'Tis been the ruin of too many good men in this man's army. Look at our commanding officer."

"Captain Ross?" Shields sneered. "Was he ever a good man?"

"Aye, sir, he was," O'Braugh said quietly. "At Franklin, Tennessee, when he was a lieutenant, all but three in his platoon were killed. He held his position until the rebels were turned away. I'd say he was a good man. And at Gaines Mill, when he led a cavalry raid that freed more than one hundred Union prisoners, I'd say he was a good man there, too." He peered at Shields steadily, hoping his words would have some impact on the man.

O'Braugh's information about Captain Ross surprised Shields. He pushed the glass of whiskey away. "I didn't know that about him," he said.

"No, sir, and that's the tragedy of drink. All the good a man has done is drowned by the liquor so that people look at him and no longer see the good—only the bad. And it's not just our captain. There's many a good soldier, commissioned and enlisted, whose judgment and character have been ruined by liquor. Don't let it happen to you, lad, no matter what your disappointments may be. Keep the ideal of your father in your mind. 'Tis far better to model yourself after him than after Captain Ross."

"Thank you for your concern, Sergeant Major," Shields said. He poured himself a cup of coffee and took a drink of the strong brew.

O'Braugh smiled. He had taken a risk in talking to an officer the way he had spoken to the lieutenant, but he believed now that it was paying off. He sighed deeply. At least he had not been severely chastised.

"But you're wasting your time. I've already composed a letter to Brigadier General Schuyler Hamilton, requesting an immediate appointment to his staff. Miss Hamilton is carrying the letter with her."

O'Braugh was stunned. "You've . . . you've used your relationship with the general's daughter to request a transfer away from here?" he stammered.

"I have." Shields looked at him defiantly.

O'Braugh sighed and looked sadly at Shields. "I was wrong in thinking you were beginning to show signs of true leadership. Lieutenant, you shame your father."

Shields slammed his fist on the table. "I told you, I'll not have his name brought up to me again! I'm me! Can't you get that through your thick head, you dumb Irish immigrant! I don't need you to remind me of my duty! I spent four years in the finest military academy in the world, learning about duty."

"Aye, sir," O'Braugh said, anger sparking inside him. "And if truth be told, 'tis four years wasted, for you've learned nothing if you'd trade upon your relationship to shirk your duty."

"Shirk my duty?"

"Aye, sir, shirk your duty. You do recall the young lieutenant who was killed at Webb's ranch, don't you?"

"What about him?"

"He had no one to call on," O'Braugh said. "He served his time. He gave his last measure of devotion, because he learned the meaning of the word 'duty'. What's the motto of that fancy school you went to, sir? 'Duty, honor, country'? If they could see you now."

Angrily, Shields swept everything off the table, and the coffeepot and cups hit the floor with a crash. The coffee spilled, ran across the wide-plank floor, and then dripped down between the cracks.

"Don't you instruct me on duty," Shields snarled, his face red with rage. "How dare you, an enlisted man, quote duty, honor, and country to me? Put up your hands, Sergeant Major." Shields stood up and raised his fists. "Put up your hands! I intend to teach you a lesson you won't soon forget!"

"I'll not be taking a swing at an officer, sir. For all I know, you'd use that as an excuse to put me away for five years," O'Braugh said, as he rose from his chair.

"I give you my word as an officer and a gentleman, I'll not press charges," Shields said.

"Your word, sir? From a man who doesn't know the meaning of the word 'duty'?"

"Damn your thick hide!" Shields said. He swung at O'Braugh, but O'Braugh blocked the punch. Shields swung again, and once more O'Braugh blocked the punch, though this time he had to step back out of the way.

"Lieutenant, you're out of order, sir!" O'Braugh shouted at him.

"Damn you! Swing back!" Shields demanded. "Swing back!" Shields swung a third time.

O'Braugh shrugged. If anyone looked in on them now, he would be just as guilty as if he had been fighting, so reluctantly he threw a punch back. He connected with Shields's chin, and Shields went down.

"Now, let that be a lesson to you, Lieutenant," he began. But to his surprise Shields was on his feet and charging at him like an angry bull. Whereas Shields's first three punches had been totally ineffective, O'Braugh's counterpunch had partially sobered Shields. The man who came at O'Braugh now was not the easy drunk that O'Braugh had put down with one punch. O'Braugh caught a fist in the side of his head. He saw stars, and his knees buckled.

The two men went at each other then, trading blows on a nearly equal basis. Neither man made any attempt to pull his punches, and since both were big and muscular, they were doing considerable damage to each other. All alone, with not even Wang as a witness, the two men fought. The fight was like some bizarre dance—two men pushing, struggling, swinging—unobserved, in the back room of the sutler's store. It was unlike any barroom fight O'Braugh had ever seen or been in. There were no cheers, no shouts of encouragement or derision from onlookers. The only sounds were those of scraping furniture, heavy breathing, and the slapping thump of fist against flesh.

Shields was younger, but O'Braugh was a little larger. Under normal circumstances, Shields might have been in a little better shape, but he had been drinking. Though he had sobered considerably from the time the fight began, he was still showing some effects of the alcohol. Shields had another disadvantage: He had been taught the manly art of self-defense as a cadet at West Point, but his lessons had been for gentleman fighters.

O'Braugh was older and experienced in barroom brawls. He used his experience to put an end to the fight before anyone came in and saw what was going on. When he saw his opening, he took it, dropping the lieutenant to the floor.

Shields tried to get up, but he fell back against the wall, slid down, and then sat there, groggily rubbing his bruised chin. He stared up at O'Braugh, breathing hard.

"I'll be leavin' now, Lieutenant," O'Braugh said, struggling to catch his breath. "If you want to get drunk, do it. I'll not be tryin' to save you from yourself. And if you'll be wantin' to send the guards after me, I'll be in my quarters."

O'Braugh stalked out of the room, leaving Shields dazed on the floor. He hoped he had beaten a little sense into the young man, but he could not be sure. He also had a sick sensation in the pit of his stomach. If Shields wanted to turn him in, there would be little he could do to defend himself in a trial by court-martial.

Two hours later a clerk from the orderly room came to the drill field to summon O'Braugh.

"The cap'n wants to see you, Sergeant Major."

"Any idea what it's about?" O'Braugh gave him a penetrating look.

"No. Lieutenant Shields is with him, though."

O'Braugh took a deep breath and exhaled slowly. He wondered if Shields had reported the fight. If so, it was the end of O'Braugh's career. Worse, it would be the end of his freedom, for he was certain to go to prison.

"Thank you, soldier. Tell the captain I'll be right there," O'Braugh said. He had used his kerchief to wipe the dust and sweat from his brow, so he decided he ought to stop by his quarters to get a clean one. While there, he also replaced his soiled service hat with a freshly blocked one. If he was going to be told that his career was over, he was going to hear it looking like a soldier.

A moment later Sergeant Major Kevin O'Braugh knocked on the door of Captain Ross's office.

"Come in, Sergeant Major," Ross barked.

O'Braugh stepped through the door and saluted sharply. He saw Lieutenant Shields standing near the map on the orderly room wall. The lieutenant was wearing a fresh uniform and was well-groomed himself. He was studying the map and did not look around at O'Braugh.

"Ah, Sergeant Major, thank you for coming," Ross said. He pointed to Shields. "The young lieutenant has come to me with a request. Since it concerns you, I thought you should be here while we discussed it."

"Yes, sir," O'Braugh said. This was it. Lieutenant Shields had requested O'Braugh's court-martial.

"What the lieutenant proposes is that . . . well, suppose I let him tell you."

Shields turned around and looked at O'Braugh. Then he cleared his throat.

"Sergeant Major, I've been giving a lot of thought to Manitoro."

It was not what O'Braugh expected to hear, and for a long moment he was silent. When he finally spoke, he realized that he had been holding his breath. "Manitoro?" he asked.

"Yes. I'd like to find him," Shields said.

"Perhaps I'd better explain," Ross interrupted. "It's no secret by now that the wedding has been canceled. All of us share the lieutenant's disappointment, of course, so I guess you can understand the lieutenant's desire to get away from the post for a while. And I, for one, want to commend him for using duty to keep his mind off his disappointment. I'm sure you agree."

"Yes, sir," O'Braugh said. "I agree completely." He was pleasantly surprised by the direction the conversation was taking. He had come here fully expecting to be in trouble because of the fight, but it was obvious that Captain Ross knew absolutely nothing about what had taken place in the back room of the sutler's store. He glanced at Shields's jaw and saw that it was not discolored.

"I'm glad you agree, Sergeant Major," Shields said. "Because I would like you to go with me as my second in command."

"You want me?" O'Braugh was stunned.

"Yes, if you don't mind." Shields smiled disarmingly. "You see, I think I have quite a bit to learn yet, and I can think of no one better suited to teach me than an experienced noncommissioned officer. Someone like yourself."

Captain Ross chuckled. "I have to say, Sergeant Major,

that the young man does seem to be showing remarkable intelligence for a second lieutenant. It generally takes the shavetails a year or more to figure that out."

"He comes from good stock," O'Braugh said, relaxing completely and smiling broadly. "And with the captain's permission, sir, I would be honored to go along as Lieutenant Shields's second in command."

"Permission granted," Ross said. He stroked his chin and leaned back in his chair. "Maybe this'll satisfy Branson."

"I beg your pardon, sir?" O'Braugh asked.

Ross waved his hand, as if erasing what he had said. "Nothing, pay no attention to me. I was merely mumbling, that's all. Farley Branson has been most vocal about my solving the Indian problem, as you may know. I was just musing that he might appreciate this patrol. Of course, he is only a civilian, and I refuse to react to anything he might have to say." Ross walked over to look at the map and turned to Shields. "Well, Lieutenant, where do you think you would like to lead this patrol?"

Shields lifted a finger to the map and began tracing a line across it. "I thought I'd head first for Sedona, then over Black Mesa, across the Verde River, and through Chino Pass down to Prescott."

"What do you think, O'Braugh?" Ross asked, turning to the sergeant major.

"I think the lieutenant has laid out a pretty good search area," O'Braugh said, nodding his approval. "That covers the most likely places for hidden camps."

"And I concur. Take whatever men and rations you need," Ross said, turning back to Shields.

"Thank you, sir," Shields said, saluting sharply. O'Braugh also saluted, and the two men left the captain's office together. A moment later, under the sally port, Shields turned to O'Braugh.

"Thank you for agreeing to go with me," he said.

"I'm honored you asked for me," O'Braugh said with a nod.

Shields rubbed his chin and smiled. "And, though I never want to speak of it again, thanks for knocking a little sense into me."

O'Braugh cleared his throat nervously. "My, uh, pleasure, sir," he said, and a broad grin broke across his handsome face.

Shields laughed heartily. "Yes, I guess it was. Now, if you would, Sergeant Major, select a dozen men for the patrol. I'd like to leave within the hour."

"We'll be ready, sir."

On a flat rock approximately twenty miles from Fort Verde, Manitoro squatted on his haunches and looked over the rim of the valley to the distant cliffs. In the brilliant afternoon sun, the world looked as if it had been painted in hues of beige, orange, and burnt ochre. From this vantage point he had a view of the entire valley, and he smiled to himself, secure in the knowledge that no one could come close to his encampment unseen.

Behind Manitoro, in a wickiup in the heart of the camp, Manitoro's father, Kelaithe, lay resting from the hot afternoon sun. Kelaithe could do this without ridicule, because he was the oldest person in the camp. He had fought the Spanish years ago when they came to dig gold out of the sacred mountains of Usen—the mountain range the whites now called Superstition Mountain, always referring to it in the singular, though it was actually a range. Kelaithe had also fought with Cochise and Nana, and even with Chatoma, before Chatoma had surrendered to the whites. Kelaithe had fought to stop the white man's wagon trains from crossing his land, and he had fought the railroads and the army. He was old and brittle now, but Manitoro could remember when Kelaithe was young and strong and frightening.

As Manitoro studied the valley before him, he suddenly realized that he was not alone. Kelaithe was there behind him, though Manitoro had not heard him approach. He was surprised that the old warrior could step so lightly as to approach him without being heard, but he did not show his surprise. He did not want to appear to be less than vigilant. Kelaithe was now sitting cross-legged on the ground, looking at Manitoro with deep, dark eyes that somehow seemed to penetrate to his very soul.

"I like to come here," Manitoro said, startled by his presence and speaking merely to overcome his awkwardness.

The old man did not answer.

"From here I can look out over the entire valley. If the

soldiers come, I will see them long before there is any danger." Manitoro spoke self-consciously, but still the old man did not answer.

"Of course, I do not expect the soldiers to come," Manitoro said. He was very uncomfortable now, and the more he tried to cover it, the more obvious it became.

"You have chosen your encampment well," Kelaithe said.

"The words of such a great warrior are flattering," Manitoro replied, relieved that Kelaithe had finally spoken. "I am honored that you speak well of your son."

"I am pleased that you have become who you have become," Kelaithe said. For just a moment, the serenity left his face, and he showed a slight anxiety. "But in so doing, I may have altered the order of things. Perhaps the stream of your life was meant to go in another direction."

"No," Manitoro said. He beat his fist upon his chest. "I am Manitoro. This is as it should be, and I would want to be no other."

"You say you have no regrets. Yet you are troubled."

"Why do you say I am troubled?"

"I know this to be so. You are troubled by the vision you had of the soldier drawing water from the flames," Kelaithe said.

"What? How . . . how did you know of that vision?" Manitoro gasped. "I have told no one."

"It is not necessary for you to speak of it. I know it is so."

"You . . . you have the power to read the thoughts of others?" Manitoro asked. "How can this be? I know you are a very wise man, but not even the Gan dancers have the power to read the thoughts of others."

"It is a power that will come to all when their time arrives," Kelaithe said. There was something different about him, though Manitoro had no idea what it was.

"Have you the power to look into the future?" Manitoro stammered.

"Yes."

Manitoro smiled broadly. "What is in my future?" he asked. He turned away from the old man and looked out over the valley again, at the play of sunlight upon the distant peaks.

"This I cannot say," Kelaithe said. "For to know your

future is to be frightened by it. And if you are frightened by your future, you will be unable to live for today."

"You speak in riddles, old man," Manitoro said, and he turned angrily, ready to demand that Kelaithe share the secret of his future with him. To his surprise, Kelaithe was gone. When the young warrior looked back toward the encampment, his father was nowhere to be seen. There was an open distance of at least fifty yards between the rock and the camp, and he wondered how Kelaithe could have covered the distance so quickly and disappeared so completely. After all, he was an old man, and he walked, when he walked, only with pain and difficulty.

Suddenly two men came out of Kelaithe's wickiup. One of them started walking toward the string of horses tied to a tree at the edge of the camp. He raised his rifle and shot a gray horse. Manitoro gasped. The horse belonged to Kelaithe. It was the custom to kill the horse of a warrior when the warrior died, so that the soul of the horse could join the soul of its owner.

The other man walked quickly toward Manitoro. "Manitoro, I am sorry to tell you that Kelaithe, your father, is dead."

"But . . . when? When did he die?" Manitoro stammered.

"A short time ago. The purifying ceremony has already been completed. You can come into the wickiup now."

The purifying ceremony, Manitoro knew, took at least as long as it takes the sun to travel the width of a hand, about half an hour by the reckoning of the white man. But that was not possible—Kelaithe could not have died half an hour ago—he was just here!

"Did you see someone with me? An old man?" Manitoro asked urgently.

"When?" asked the startled warrior.

"Now. Just before you came," Manitoro answered sharply.

"No. I saw you up here alone, and I knew you were with your thoughts. I did not disturb you before, because I knew Kelaithe would not want me to."

"But he was here!" Manitoro exclaimed.

"Who was here?"

Manitoro raised his arm and started to point toward the wickiup; then he dropped it. He realized that the visit was for his eyes only. He felt the hair stand up on the back of his neck, and he turned and looked out over the valley. He had another vision. There, riding through the sky, he saw the gray horse and the painted figure of the man who had been so frightening to Manitoro in his youth. He saw Kelaithe, not as a man withered by age and drawn with pain, but as a warrior with eternal youth.

"Tell the others," Manitoro said. "We will make a war party to honor my father."

Chapter Six

Emily Rourke sat on top of the stagecoach at the Prescott train station and watched while Susan Hamilton boarded the train. The young woman tossed her head haughtily and upbraided the porter for the way he was carrying the train case she would keep with her during the journey. Emily clucked her tongue and shook her head.

"'Course it ain't none of my business," Sergeant Keogh said conspiratorially as he leaned toward Emily to speak with her. Sitting on his horse beside the coach, he was meticulously carving a plug of chewing tobacco. When he was satisfied with his handiwork, he stuck it in his mouth and then put the tobacco and knife away. "But if you was to ask me," he continued, "I'd say the young lieutenant's a whole heap better off without that woman."

"I agree with you on both points, Martin. Lieutenant Shields is better off without her," Emily turned her head to look pointedly at the sergeant "—and it's none of your business."

Keogh chuckled. "Don't go worryin' yourself about that, Mrs. Rourke," he said. "I didn't come into the army yesterday, you know. I got better sense than to try an' tell some lovesick young buck the woman he's stuck on is no good for him. Especially if that lovesick young buck is an officer."

The train whistle shrieked, startling Emily and stopping her from commenting further. The engineer opened the throttle valve, and steam gushed from the wheel cylinders and billowed across the platform like fog cloaking a marsh. The piston rod moved the driver wheel, and the train jerked forward. Two more whistle blasts sounded, and the train eased out of the station.

Wondering if Susan would wave good-bye, or at least take one last look at the town she had visited so briefly, Emily watched as the cars moved by slowly. When the car that carried Susan came abreast with her, Emily could see the young woman through the window sitting rigidly in her seat, staring straight ahead. That image lasted but a moment, then the train was gone.

"Excuse me, Mrs. Rourke. Will you be making your regular run to Sedona?"

Shaking her head to clear the picture of Susan Hamilton from her mind, Emily looked down from her seat on the coach at the speaker, a tall, slender man with a white handlebar mustache. He was Tom Murchison, the ticket agent for the railroad.

"Hello, Tom," she said with a smile. "Yes, I suppose I will. Have you got some passengers for me?"

"I sure do. Two businessmen from back East, a school marm, and a man and wife."

"Sounds like a profitable load," Emily said, nodding her head. "Send them down to the stage depot. I'll leave as soon as I can change teams."

"Uh, one of the passengers is worried about Indians," Tom said.

"I'll be taking a shotgun guard with me," Emily said.

"And an army escort," Sergeant Keogh put in quickly.

"Martin, do you think you should?" Emily asked in surprise. "I appreciate it, of course, but I don't want to get you in trouble."

"The way I look at it, Mrs. Rourke, the reason we're out here is to protect civilians, and you're a civilian."

Emily chuckled. "I am that, all right."

"Besides, the way O'Braugh feels about you, he'd probably skin me alive if he found out I let his sweetheart make the trip without escort."

"His sweetheart?" Emily blushed. "Does he think that?"

"Yes, ma'am. He don't say it out loud, but there's not a man on that post that don't know the sergeant major's sweet on you."

"Go on, Martin," Emily said, embarrassed by this revelation. "You talk too much."

"Just speakin' true, that's all," Keogh said. He twisted in his saddle and looked at his men. "If you don't have any objection, I'm goin' to let the men have one beer each while you're gettin' the team changed."

"I don't mind at all," Emily said. "In fact, tell them I said to charge the beers to me."

Sergeant Keogh smiled broadly. "Why, thank you, that's mighty kind."

As the stage wheels rolled over the packed dirt road with a soft, rhythmic crunch, the late-afternoon sun was edging toward the western horizon. Emily rode high on the driver's seat, looking out over the broad backs of the six horses at the familiar countryside. In the distance she could see two of the escort riders who had ranged about a quarter of a mile away from the road. Beside her rode the shotgun guard, a new man she had hired just last week. He was a taciturn, weathered man, whose lips were hidden by a bushy moustache. His eyes were dark brown and penetrating. He had not spoken a word since they left Prescott, which was all right with Emily because she preferred silence while she was driving. It gave her time for her own thoughts.

They had just passed the halfway point between Prescott and Sedona when one of the military escort riders came galloping toward the coach.

"Sarge, I seen Indians ahead!" he cried breathlessly as he reached them.

"Get 'em rollin', Mrs. Rourke!" Keogh shouted. Emily cracked her whip over the heads of the team. They responded immediately, and the stage lurched and began rolling at a brisk clip.

The guard jacked a shell into the chamber, braced himself with a knee on the seat, and scanned the distant ridges. "There they are," he shouted, pointing to a ridgeline off to the right. Emily could see no more than six Indians, and even though they were several hundred yards away, she could see that they were painted for war. Riding in a line parallel with the stage, they were bent low over their ponies and were urging them on. One of them fired a long-range shot toward the stage, and the shotgun guard returned the fire.

They rode along for several minutes, and to her surprise the Indians made no effort to come any closer. Emily began to breathe a little more easily when she realized that the Indians had no intention of doing anything more than harassing the stage, possibly because there were too few of them to give them the advantage they wanted.

"I'm going to slow the horses before I tire them," Emily shouted. "I don't think they're going to come any closer."

"I wish they would," the shotgun guard answered. "We could take care of them."

"Emily, look!" Keogh suddenly shouted, using her first name in his excitement. She glanced ahead to see what had caused his concern and was horrified to see two much larger groups of Indians approaching the stage from the ridges on each side of the road. "That first bunch was just leadin' us into a trap."

"That there's Manitoro!" The shotgun guard glared at the lead rider of the group attacking on their left. He fired at Manitoro but missed.

Though Emily had just slowed the horses, she whipped them up again, this time urging them to all-out speed. She knew they would not be able to sustain the pace for very long, but she had no choice.

This time, the Indians had no intention of merely harassing them. Pressing in from all sides, they were gradually squeezing in on the stage. Within another few minutes, they would have the coach completely surrounded.

"I got one of the bastards!" the shotgun guard yelled. The words were no sooner out of his mouth than Emily heard the angry buzz of a bullet, followed by the sound of it hitting flesh. Stunned by the impact, the guard dropped his rifle, and though Emily reached for it, she was unable to catch it before it tumbled overboard. Beside her the guard sank back to the seat, clutching at his shoulder as blood streamed through his fingers.

"Sarge! They hit Bryans!"

Hearing the shout, Emily glanced around to see a soldier reeling in his saddle as he fell. A couple of Indians closed in on the fallen man, and Emily looked away so she would not have to watch what they did to him. Repelled, she felt the bile of fear rising in her throat, and she knew that it was all over for them.

A new body of men suddenly swept over a nearby ridge, and Emily's heart jumped for joy when she saw the small, red-and-white swallowtail guidon. Almost at the same moment, she recognized Kevin O'Braugh, riding in front of the charging cavalry alongside Lieutenant Shields.

"Martin, look!" she exclaimed happily, pointing at the advancing cavalry.

"We've got them now!" Keogh shouted. "Men, follow me!" Keogh led his soldiers away from the racing coach toward the Indians. With Keogh's small group suddenly attacking on one side, and Shields's larger group on the other, Emily watched as Manitoro and his warriors were caught in a cross fire.

Emily had spent enough time in Indian country alongside the army to know something about the way the Apache fought. They followed rules that had been laid down generations before, and they never deviated from them. Manitoro had learned his battle tactics from Kelaithe, and Kelaithe had learned them from Nana and Cochise. The principles of engagement they followed were absolute. You did not engage in battle unless you had absolute superiority. Although Manitoro had more warriors than there were soldiers, the soldiers were well armed, well trained, and well led. As a result, Manitoro did not have absolute superiority. Emily knew that Manitoro would order a withdrawal and that none of his braves would question him.

As she watched the Apaches turn their horses and gallop toward the ridges, Emily pulled her coach to a halt, not only to let the horses catch their breath, but to allow her to care for the wounded shotgun guard. Below her, she could hear her passengers opening the doors of the coach and climbing out, cheering the soldiers as they pursued the Indians.

Glancing up from the wounded guard's shoulder, Emily saw Lieutenant Shields and his patrol chase Manitoro's raiding party to the foot of the ridgeline. As the Apaches disappeared among the ridges, the lieutenant held up his hand to halt the pursuit. She could hear the barking shouts of the men being ordered back to the stagecoach.

In a few moments Emily looked up to see Kevin O'Braugh and Mark Shields riding toward the coach. O'Braugh dismounted immediately and hurried toward Emily, his concern for her easily read in his face.

"Emily, are you all right?" he asked.

"Yes, but my guard is wounded, and one of the soldiers was killed."

Shields looked questioningly at Keogh.

"It was Bryans, sir," Keogh said.

"The young man from St. Louis," Shields said sadly, shaking his head.

"Yes, sir," Keogh answered. From the expression on his face Emily knew that Keogh was favorably impressed that the lieutenant knew Bryans.

"I'll write a letter to his parents," Shields said. "Any other men wounded?"

"A few flesh wounds is all."

"Lieutenant, we'd best get this lad back to the post so Doc Hartfield can treat him," O'Braugh said after looking at the shotgun guard.

"All right," Shields said. "We'll terminate the patrol now and accompany the stage back. Sergeant, move the guard into the coach."

Throughout the trip back to the fort Lieutenant Shields rode close to the coach. About half an hour after they had left the scene of the attack, O'Braugh rode up alongside Shields to talk to him.

"Lieutenant, we're close enough to the fort now that Sergeant Keogh could take them on in." He pointed off to the north. "Across that second ridgeline lies Chatoma's village. It might be a good idea to go talk with him. To tell you the truth, sir, I had no idea Manitoro's band had gotten so large. Maybe he can tell us a little about it."

Shields twisted around in his saddle and looked back toward the escort detail. The wounded seemed to be riding easily, and the soldiers riding guard seemed confident and poised. He glanced up at Emily, who smiled down at him and nodded. "Good idea, Sergeant Major," he said. "Turn the command over to Sergeant Keogh, and we'll go have a talk with this man Chatoma."

Sasha Quiet Stream was sitting in Chatoma's tent next to the sickly old chief when she heard her name being called. She was startled, for she did not hear her name spoken often. Though the Apache used names when they were speaking of a third party, they rarely addressed someone directly by name, except on very special occasions. Names were used at important times in a person's life. Names could also be used to summon aid when there was a particular danger. By custom, an Apache would never refuse to help another, if the help was requested by calling him by name. Even a woman's brother would address her as "my sister," and a father would call her "my daughter." There were some exceptions to this. A warrior who had proven himself by brave deeds or a woman who had proven herself by her wisdom or her compassion would allow himself or herself to be called by name, because sharing the name with others was sharing the power. The theory was that a man or woman who had risen to a position of great importance had so much power that it could not be diluted by the mere sharing of a name.

During the summer of Sasha's sixteenth year, she had had a great deal of time to reflect on that and on the other customs of the People. That summer, she, as was expected of her, had gone to the mountains to complete a one-week's sojourn in preparation of the ceremony of her becoming a woman. Not only was it expected of her, but she expected it of herself; for she no longer thought of herself as Lily Mason, but as Sasha Quiet Stream. Sasha had accepted the People, and she had been accepted by them as one of their own, though Chatoma had made her aware of the ways of the whites. No one had ever exhibited the slightest prejudice toward her because of her fair skin, yellow hair, and eyes the color of the sky. However, she was teased for her size. She was not as stout or as strong as most Apache women. She was taller and much slimmer, with delicate features unlike the stolid, moon-faced girls who were her peers. Her adoptive parents had worried about her physical abnormalities and wondered aloud if all white girls were so cursed. The tribal midwife had examined her, however, and declared that despite her slimness, her full breasts and rounded thighs were generous enough to allow her to have babies.

For that one-week's sojourn during the summer of her sixteenth year, she had been left alone to wander through the wilderness, seeking her own water and food and relying on her wits to keep her safe. During that period a great portion of each day had been set aside for reflection and meditation. She had thought of her youth, and the memories of being a young girl raised in an Apache camp had been far stronger images than the fuzzy, almost unrecalled time before. She could hardly remember the wagon train and was only barely aware of the white man and woman who had been her father and mother or the boy who had been her brother. She could remember nothing before the wagon train, but she could recall that they were going to California. She still did not know exactly where California was, though she dimly knew that it was to have been a happy place. If that were so, then she thought maybe she was in California, for her life had been a happy one.

There had been times of sorrow, of course. The year after she became a woman, her Indian mother had died. Now Chatoma, her Indian father, was suffering from some sickness that the medicine men of the village could not cure. They had mixed herbs and burned totems, but still the illness lingered.

As she contemplated all these things, she listened to his labored breathing, and she dipped a cloth into a gourd of water. She did not know if it was helping, but she felt that she had to do something. The water rippled as she withdrew the cloth, and she put it on her father's head.

Behind her, the tent flap opened, and the person who had spoken her name stuck his head through the opening.

"Soldiers come," the brave whispered.

"How many?" she asked softly.

"Two."

Sasha left her father's side and went out to meet them. One was O'Braugh. Sasha knew him well, knew him to be a good man. The other was the young lieutenant she had met at the Webb ranch. She remembered him as being very handsome, and now she saw that her memory had not lied.

"I am pleased that you have visited me, O'Braugh," Sasha said with a smile. She looked at Shields. "And you have brought your friend."

"Sasha, this is Lieutenant Mark Shields," O'Braugh said.

Sasha immediately stuck her hand out and smiled broadly. "Do you see?" she said proudly. "I remember the ways of the whites. I remember that you shake hands when you meet someone."

Shields took her hand and looked into her eyes. He mumbled a faint hello.

"We have come to speak with your father," O'Braugh said.

"You have heard of his illness? He will be pleased," Sasha said.

"He is ill?"

"Yes, very. I have been trying to get him to go to the fort. I know that Dr. Hartfield has strong medicines that will help him. But he will not leave. Please, O'Braugh, talk to him. Make him go." Her clear blue eyes pleaded with O'Braugh.

"I'll see what I can do," O'Braugh said, frowning. "But you know your father, Sasha. He's a strong-willed man. He does only what he wants to do."

The two soldiers followed Sasha into her father's tent. Chatoma was lying on a bed of skins, looking very weak, breathing in raspy gasps. When he saw them, he tried to sit up.

"No, Chief, you stay there and rest," O'Braugh said, holding his hand out. "We'll sit beside you."

"You honor me," Chatoma said weakly.

Sasha began gently bathing his forehead again.

"Chief, we'd like to ask you some questions about Manitoro," O'Braugh began.

"I will answer if I can," Chatoma whispered.

"His band seems larger than it was before."

Chatoma nodded his head slowly. "Yes. I am sorry to say that his numbers grow larger."

"Where are they coming from? Are the young men leaving your camp?" O'Braugh asked, frowning in concern.

"No," Chatoma said. "My warriors are good men. They make no war against the whites."

"He's getting them from somewhere."

"Yes. Many warriors have been driven out of the place you call New Mexico. They have no place to go, so they have joined with Manitoro."

"How many?" Shields asked.

"Enough," Chatoma answered. And though neither soldier asked him to clarify his answer, he did so anyway. "Enough that Manitoro may soon feel he can stop the raids and make war."

"Damn," O'Braugh swore softly. "That's not good."

"I see dark times ahead, my friend," Chatoma said sadly;

his words were barely audible. "I see dark times for the whites, and dark times for my people. Manitoro will make war, and when he does, the soldiers will fight back."

"Of course we will fight back," Shields said quickly.

"When the soldiers fight back, they will not see the people of Manitoro and the people of Chatoma. They will see only Indians, and all will look alike. My people will be set upon by Manitoro and the whites," he said sadly. He shook his head wearily.

"Maybe not," O'Braugh said. "Maybe we can work together and keep your people safe."

"I hope this can be done," Chatoma said. "But I fear it will not be." He coughed, a deep, racking cough that lasted for several moments before the spell passed.

"Chief, why don't you come to the fort with us? I'm sure Dr. Hartfield can treat your illness," O'Braugh urged.

"I cannot go," Chatoma said. "These are hard times now. I must stay with my people."

Sasha began talking to him urgently in his own language. She knew that she had to persuade him to go. The People needed him well and strong to face the terrible threat that Manitoro and his warriors presented. She spoke for several moments. Then at last she looked up at Shields and smiled.

"My father has agreed to go, if I may go with him."

"Yes," Shields said. "Yes, of course you can go with him."

"Then I shall have a travois prepared, and we can leave." She smiled warmly. "It will be good to see my friends the Hartfields again."

Half an hour later Shields, O'Braugh, Sasha, and her father were on their way to the fort. Sasha rode the horse that pulled the travois, while Chatoma lay on the device, traveling comfortably.

As they walked the horses in the last light of the day, Shields felt a peacefulness overcome him. He reflected on the events of the afternoon and on the beautiful and gentle young woman riding near him. When she had shaken his hand, he had been mesmerized. It was strange, he thought; she was the one living as an Indian, yet it was he who felt brutish, almost savage, next to her. The delicate way she tended to the ailing Chatoma had touched him deeply. When she spoke the Apache tongue to the man she called her father, the language Shields had thought so harsh and guttural before rippled over her tongue and tinkled like a wind chime as it passed her lips.

As he looked over at her now, the last deep red rays of the sun glimmered on her long blond hair. She seemed to feel his eyes on her, for she turned to smile at him in a soft, serene way.

Shields found himself so captivated by the image of the beautiful woman, the Indian horse, and the travois that he felt he had to record it. He reached into his saddlebag and pulled out a pad and charcoal pencil. Then, hooking his leg across the pommel of his saddle, he began sketching the scene as they rode toward the post.

Chapter Seven

When Shields and his party reached the fort, he learned from the sentry at the gate that the coach and its escort detail had already arrived and that the wounded men had been taken to the post hospital. The first thing Shields did was make arrangements to have Chatoma taken to Dr. Hartfield. After that, he went to headquarters and made a full report to Captain Ross, telling him the details of the attack on the stagecoach.

"Another soldier killed," Ross said angrily. "And still they won't give me the reinforcements I ask for." Ross walked over to a shelf and took down a bottle to pour himself a drink. Since it was after regular duty hours, the captain seemed to feel no need to justify the drink. He held the bottle toward Shields in silent invitation.

"Thank you, no," Shields said, holding up his hand to stop Ross. "I have a few things to do yet."

"I suppose I do, too," Ross said with a deep sigh. "I need to write a letter to the young man's family."

"If you don't mind, I would like to do that," Shields volunteered.

"No, I don't mind at all," Ross said, glancing up. Relief was plainly written on his face. "In fact, I would appreciate that. I've written enough letters of that sort in my career. By the way, I suppose you noticed that the coach is still here, that it didn't go on to Sedona."

"Yes, sir, I saw that."

"By the time they got here, it was already too late for

94

them to go on. I gave Mrs. Rourke permission to stay over-night, and I've made arrangements for the passengers. To-morrow, we'll send an escort detail to take the coach on in to Sedona."

"That's a good idea," Shields agreed. "Especially since Manitoro's band has grown so much larger."

"And I'm expected to handle it with one augmented cavalry troop," Ross said disgustedly. He poured himself another drink. "Lieutenant Shields, how well do you know General Hamilton?"

"General Hamilton? He is the Army Inspector General. I met him when he came to West Point . . . and, of course, through his daughter. He is going to be my father-in-law, so I suppose you could say that I know him quite well."

"Well enough that he will respond to a personal request from you?" Ross narrowed his eyes as he peered at Shields.

"You're talking about my request for transfer to his staff?"

"Yes," Ross said. "And something else," he added pointedly.

"What else, sir?" Shields asked cautiously.

"I thought perhaps if you, personally, wrote a letter to General Hamilton, explaining the difficulty of our position out here, he might carry the message to the War Depart-ment. With his intercession on our behalf, they might well send me another troop of cavalry."

Such personal requests that circumvented normal chan-nels were, Shields knew, very much frowned upon. He ran his hand through his hair nervously. "Well, I, uh . . ." he stammered.

"Never mind, I understand," Ross interrupted brusquely. "If you tell him in one letter how badly we need reinforce-ments, while in another letter you are asking to be reas-signed, it does not look good for you."

"I wasn't thinking of that," Shields said, though he knew there was a great deal of truth in what Ross was saying. "I'll write the letter if you think it will do any good."

"Never mind. Perhaps Connell and Trapman can write the letters for me." Ross frowned thoughtfully.

"Connell and Trapman? Who are they?"

"Oh, you didn't get the chance to meet them, did you? They are the two businessmen who were on the coach when it was attacked. They are over in the sutler's store now, visiting with Branson, who tells me they are very important railroad builders. I'd like to know what they think about what's going on out here." Ross poured himself another drink and then looked up at Shields. "That's all, Lieutenant. You're dismissed."

"Yes, sir." As Shields left the headquarters building, he glanced over at the sutler's store. It was nearly dark now, and the lamps in the store were already glowing. He considered going over there for a drink but, remembering this morning's unpleasant episode with alcohol, decided he had drunk enough for one day. Instead, he went to his quarters to write the letter to Private Timothy Bryans's parents.

There were at least a dozen soldiers in the back room of the sutler's store. Half of them had been on the patrol with Shields, while the others had remained in the garrison all day. The men who had gone on patrol were regaling the garrison troopers with stories of the day's adventure, each vying with the others to express, as humorously as possible, how frightened he had been during the peak of the action.

"Why, I was so scairt, I couldn't even work up a spit," one of the soldiers said.

"I was so scairt, I didn't have to spit," another added. "Water was comin' out the other end, if you know what I mean."

The men sitting around the table burst into loud laughter at his observation.

In the back of the room, at a table set apart from the others, Farley Branson paused at the outburst of laughter and then resumed his conversation with Connell and Trapman. Though the businessmen would be staying in Sedona, they had come to the West to meet with Branson. The fact that they had ended up at Fort Verde was most fortuitous, and they lost no time in transacting their business. However, as Branson soon noticed, it was not a smooth transaction. Both men were angry and frightened over the experience they had had on the stagecoach that afternoon. Connell was expressing his opinion rather forcefully.

"The soldiers can laugh about it, but I can't. If you think our company is going to invest money in a railroad line that would run right through the heart of savage Indian country, then you have another think coming."

"We could have been scalped," Trapman put in, rubbing his nearly bald head gingerly.

"Gentlemen, gentlemen, I assure you, all this will soon be settled," Branson said smoothly as he poured another glass of whiskey for each of them. "I have it on very good authority that the Indian problem is about to be settled, once and for all."

"How?"

"Why, in the same way it has been settled all over the West," Branson explained confidently. "The army is going to launch an all-out campaign against them. By the time you are ready to build your railroad out here, there won't be any Indians left. They'll all be on reservations."

"I wish I had your confidence in that. But from what I hear in Washington, the idea seems to be appeasement where necessary," Trapman said.

"Appeasement won't work here," Branson said quickly. "The only way we are ever going to have peace is if the Indians—all of them—are forced out of here, part and parcel. Captain Ross is just about ready to order such a campaign."

"When that campaign is undertaken," Connell started to say. "No, make that, when that campaign has been successfully concluded—when the Indian threat is completely removed—then we will consider investing here."

Branson smiled broadly. "In that case, gentlemen, we should drink a toast," he said. "Because we will soon be doing business together."

"Not so fast," Trapman interjected. "There's another detail that must be attended to."

"What is that?" Branson asked.

"You understand there are hundreds of thousands of dollars involved in the building and development of a new railroad. Our investors will not risk that much money—not one dollar, not one red cent—until they have clear title to the land."

"That won't be a problem," Branson assured them. "I'll provide your company with clear title to the land."

"How can you say that? The route you have selected goes right through land deeded, by treaty, to Chatoma's people. We have been informed that they won't sell to us."

"Leave it to me, gentlemen," Branson said. "I assure you, we will have no more problems with the Indians, and I will have clear title to the right-of-way."

"You'd better," Trapman growled. "For without it, I can promise you there will be no deal."

Branson stood up. "If you'll excuse me now, gentlemen, I have some business to tend to." He pointed to the whiskey. "In the meantime, please, drink all you want. It's on the house."

Connell chuckled. "I'll say this for you, Branson. You are a good host," he said, reaching for the bottle.

Branson left the two businessmen with their whiskey and then stepped outside. Darkness had completely enveloped the fort, and the sentries were at their posts. Dim lights glowed from the NCO quarters as the married sergeants, finished with their day's duty, were just sitting down to supper. From the barracks he could hear someone softly singing a ballad, and from behind the married quarters came a squeal of laughter from the children, who were playing their nightly game of kick the can. Branson hurried across the quadrangle to Captain Ross's quarters, hoping he could catch the commanding officer before he was completely besotted.

"Enter," Ross called when Branson knocked on the door of his quarters. When Branson stepped inside, he saw Ross sitting on a sofa. The meal that had been served by his orderly lay on the table barely touched, and a bottle of whiskey sat next to it. Ross held up his half-full glass in greeting. "Hello, Branson," he slurred. "What brings you here?"

"Captain Ross, I have come to enter a citizen's complaint," Branson said firmly.

"About what?"

"About the Indian attack on the stagecoach this afternoon. I told you about the two businessmen on the coach, do you remember?" When Ross nodded, Branson went on. "Yes, well, I just left them, and I must tell you, they are in a highly agitated state—a state, I might add, that is definitely not conducive to business."

"Were they wounded?"

"No."

"Then what are they complaining about? The shotgun guard and some of my soldiers were," Ross replied angrily. "And one of my men was killed."

"Yes, I heard about that," Branson answered quickly. "I'm sorry, but it only tends to underscore the point I'm trying to make. You have lost control of the situation."

"I'd hardly say I have lost control," Ross responded indignantly.

"I would. For example, did you know I have a wagon-load of goods that should have arrived day before yesterday? I didn't say anything about it, because sometimes they are as much as a day overdue. But in view of the attack on the stagecoach, I'm now quite concerned about them. I'm afraid they may have encountered Indians."

Ross finished the liquor in his glass and then poured himself another drink. "Mr. Branson, what is the point you are trying to make?" he asked, looking up at him.

"The point, Captain Ross, is that I think the time has come for you to take action—decisive action."

"What kind of action?"

"Why that's obvious, isn't it? I believe you should round up all the Indians, good and bad, and transport them to one of the reservations near Phoenix."

Ross studied Branson over the edge of his glass for a moment. Finally he lowered the glass and spoke.

"Mr. Branson, as you know, I am not fond of Indians, good or bad. I've seen too many so-called 'good' Indians go bad, and 'bad' Indians go good when it served their purpose. If I were in absolute authority out here, I might do as you suggest. But I have no authority to do that now, especially with Chatoma. He's never given us a moment's trouble, and he's the pet of the department."

"How do we know that he's never given us any trouble?" Branson asked. "An Indian is an Indian. You heard Lieutenant Shields report that Manitoro has many more warriors than any of us believed. Who's to say they aren't coming from Chatoma's camp?"

"They're coming from New Mexico," Ross said.

"How do we know that?"

"Because Chatoma told us," Ross started and then stopped.

Branson smiled, aware that he had just made a point. "Chatoma told us," he repeated sarcastically. "And that makes it gospel?"

"We have no evidence that he is lying to us," Ross insisted.

"And no proof that he is telling the truth," Branson retorted. "All we know for certain is that Indians are raiding and killing with impunity, and the army is doing nothing about it."

"Mr. Branson, I'm doing everything that I can do," Ross protested.

"No, sir. You can do more," Branson shot back.

"Not without violating orders."

"Your primary order, I believe, is to provide for the safety of civilians. Am I not right?" Branson asked pointedly.

"Yes."

"Take my word for it, Captain. That can best be accomplished by moving against the Indians . . . all of them."

"I don't know," Ross hedged.

"Captain, you owe me," Branson said angrily. "In fact, if we were to get very specific, you owe me a great deal. I wonder what the War Department would think if I wrote them a letter about your liquor debt to me?"

"You . . . you wouldn't do that, would you?" Ross asked in a frightened tone of voice.

"Perhaps not," Branson admitted, narrowing his eyes. "Perhaps we could work out an accommodation."

"See here, are you trying to blackmail me?" Ross demanded.

"Not at all, Captain, not at all. I'm merely saying that, as a citizen who is being personally hurt by these Indian outrages, I would be very grateful to the army for doing what the army is supposed to do. And I would show my gratitude to you by throwing away the book on your liquor debt, which is, I must say, quite substantial."

"I couldn't do it for that reason," Ross protested. "That wouldn't be ethical."

"Then look at it this way," Branson went on, seizing the advantage. "Aggressive initiative now might make a favorable impression upon the War Department. If you had a successful campaign against the Indians, and if I wrote a personal letter of gratitude and influenced some of my friends to do so as well, you could very well be wearing the leaves of a major, or even lieutenant colonel, by the end of the year."

"Yes," Ross mused. "The army does, sometimes, reward boldness and daring."

"If it is successful," Branson added. "And believe me, Ross, the only way you can be certain a campaign would be successful would be to remove all the Indians from this entire area."

"I'll give your suggestion consideration, Mr. Branson," Ross said warily.

"Don't wait too long, Ross," Branson warned as he moved toward the door preparing to leave. "If you let this situation get out of hand, the War Department will send more troops out here—and a new commander to take charge."

Ross poured another drink. "Yes," he said, sipping his whiskey. "It is something that I must think about."

When the stagecoach left Fort Verde the next morning, Farley Branson noticed that it was escorted by an entire platoon. This was more than three times the size of the normal escort, but since Manitoro was getting bolder and showing more strength, a larger escort detail was needed to guarantee the safety of the coach.

Most of the fort turned out to see the coach off, since the ceremony surrounding such departures served to lighten an otherwise deadly routine. After the coach had left, the men in the garrison returned to their regular work details.

Branson waited until the day was in full swing. Then he saddled up and slipped away from the fort, unnoticed.

He had traveled less than ten miles from the fort when two Indians startled him by suddenly appearing from behind a large rock. They effectively used their horses to block Branson's path, glaring at him with eyes that were threatening and frightening. Both were armed with rifles, and Branson knew they were warriors from Manitoro's band. He reined up sharply.

For a long moment the three men stared at each other, none of them bothering to mask the hatred that was in their eyes.

Finally Branson demanded angrily, "All right, don't just sit there like dumb savages. I'm supposed to meet Manitoro here. Where is he?"

"Come," one of the Indians said, and he turned his horse to lead the way. The other warrior dropped in behind Branson as they rode through a long, narrow pass. Branson was uncomfortable, sandwiched as he was between the two Indians, but he knew that they would do nothing to harm him. If they did, they would have to answer to Manitoro, and right now, he was too valuable to the renegade leader for Manitoro to let anything happen to him.

After a while the narrow pass widened into a ravine, and Branson saw several Indians sitting around a small fire. They had just cooked a meal, whether rabbit or a small dog Branson was not sure. Whatever it was, the Indians were ripping the meat off the carcass and stuffing it into their mouths, leaving shining smears of grease on their faces and chins. To Branson it was like watching a pack of wild dogs eat, and he was revolted by it. He took a deep breath and tried not to reveal his reactions; he knew the Indians would construe them as a sign of weakness.

"Do you want food?" Manitoro asked, holding out a stringy, greasy piece of meat.

"No, thank you," Branson said, turning his head away distastefully. "I ate before I left the fort."

"White man's food? Grits, greens, taters?" Manitoro sneered disdainfully.

"Yes," Branson answered. It was easier to agree. Branson was frightened of Manitoro, though he made every effort to hide it.

"I don't like grits, greens, and taters. When do we get more guns?" he asked, abruptly changing the subject.

"I have more rifles coming," Branson said. "But you must earn them."

"What do you want me to do?"

Branson took a map from his jacket and, dropping to sit on his heels beside the savage, spread it on the ground. "Here," he said pointing to several spots. "These places, here and here. I want them attacked. I want the white men driven off."

"Yes, I will do that."

"When you have done that, I will give you more guns."

"Why do you make war against your own people?" Manitoro demanded, his blue eyes fixing Branson with a cold glare.

"I have my reasons," Branson replied. "It is not necessary that you understand. It is only necessary that you do what I tell you to do." He stood up, leaving the map spread on the earth. "Oh, and one more thing. Be careful about attacking stagecoaches in the future. There were two men on the coach you attacked yesterday who are very important to me."

"They are not important to me," Manitoro said easily, shrugging his shoulders. He took another bite of meat.

"Oh, but they are. They are the men who sell me the

guns. Without them, I can get no more guns for you. From now on, you must attack only those places I tell you to attack. Here, the places on this map—you must attack them."

Manitoro looked at the map for a moment longer. "Yes," he said. "I will attack these places."

"I must go now," Branson said. "If I am gone too long, the people at the fort will wonder where I am."

"Go," Manitoro said. He waved his hand, and the Indians who were behind Branson moved out of the way.

Manitoro watched as Branson rode back up the pass. "I do not like that white man," an Indian standing next to Manitoro said.

"It does not matter," Manitoro replied. "As long as he supplies me with guns, I will let him live. When he is of no more use, I will kill him myself."

Back at Fort Verde Sasha Quiet Stream was sitting in a chair beside her father's bed. He was in a long room filled with beds, some of which were occupied by the soldiers who had been wounded in the fight the day before. Dr. Hartfield and two soldiers, whom she heard called hospital orderlies, were tending to them.

Sasha was fascinated by the hospital, by the strange smells of medicines and ointments, by the knives, clamps, scissors, and other instruments. While she conceded that it was a good idea to bring all the sick and injured people to one place, the better to care for them, she preferred the Indian way of leaving the sick and wounded with their own families. That way, the patients would always be surrounded by people who loved them.

Mark Shields came into the hospital at that moment, and she smiled at him. She believed he was the most handsome man she had ever seen, and she wondered what it would be like to have him call on her father, bearing gifts of horses and rifles. Among her people courtships were begun in such a way. Sometimes a young brave would vie for the maid of his choice by offering the best price, but a wise and loving father would make the decision about his prospective son-in-law not on the value of the gifts, but on the desires of his daughter's heart. Sasha thought that if Mark Shields became her suitor, she would certainly let her father know the desires of her heart. It would not take many horses and rifles for her!

Suddenly she blushed. How could she be thinking such things? He had given her no sign that he would ever become her suitor. Still, she thought, it would be nice if he did, and it was a pleasant thing to think about.

Sasha watched as Shields stopped at the bed of each wounded soldier and spoke a few words. She knew that he was their chief, and she could tell from the way the men spoke that they liked him. It was a good sign for a leader to be liked by the men he led. That meant he had humility as well as power, and without actually articulating the thought, she knew that such a thing was a rare and wonderful quality.

After Shields spoke to each of his men, he came down to speak with her. She had hoped that he would.

"How is your father doing?" Shields asked, smiling warmly at her.

"He breathes more easily now," Sasha said. "I think it was good to bring him here to the white man's hospital."

"Yes, Dr. Hartfield is a skilled physician," Shields said. "I'm sure he can make your father well again." He looked at Sasha with unabashed appreciation, and when she smiled at him, he said, "You are a very beautiful young woman. I would like to do your portrait."

Sasha was thrilled that he found her beautiful, but she did not understand the word *portrait*.

"What is portrait?"

"A picture," Shields said. "I'm an artist. Here, let me show you."

Shields was carrying a small sketch pad, and he opened it to show her some of the drawings he had made. One was of Emily Rourke, sitting on the seat of the coach.

"It is Emily!" Sasha gasped, amazed at the skill that could reproduce an image so accurately.

"Yes," Shields said. He opened another page, and she saw the one he had done the day before of her riding the horse and pulling the travois. She laughed and put her hand to her mouth.

"What power you have," she exclaimed. She looked at him with a questioning gaze. "I do not understand why a man with the power to make such wonderful pictures is in the army. You should do pictures all the time."

"Ah," Shields said, closing the pad. "Now you know my secret. I would like nothing better than to become a full-time artist. I would like to just tour the West, drawing pictures of the magnificent things to be seen out here so that the people back East could know what a beautiful country we live in."

"Then why don't you?" Sasha asked. "You aren't a pony soldier who cannot quit. You are a chief. You can quit anytime you want."

"You mean resign. Yes, I can resign. But I have a responsibility to someone."

"Your father?"

Shields looked surprised. "Yes. How did you know?"

"Many times a young man who does something he does not want to do does so because it is what his father wants. Why don't you tell your father you do not wish to be in the army?"

"My father's dead," Shields said simply. He sighed. "That's the whole problem. He was a hero—a very great man. He was killed during the Civil War, and now I am expected to live up to his image. I must tell you, it is very hard to do."

Sasha looked at Chatoma, who was sleeping peacefully. "Yes," she said quietly. "I know what it is to have a father who is a very powerful man. Just like you with your father, I want to do honor to him. But that does not mean I must become a chief. I do not think you must follow in your father's footsteps to pay honor to him. It is much better that you follow your own true path."

She looked back at Shields, and her eyes were like windows to her soul. Shields had never looked so deeply into another human being before, had never felt as intimate with anyone as he was feeling with this young woman right now. It was warm and thrilling, but strangely disquieting.

"You must look inside yourself, Mark Shields, and do what your heart tells you, for that is the true source of all power."

"I, uh, must think about that," Shields said. He left the hospital feeling both touched and unsettled by his conversation with Sasha.

Thoughts of Sasha plagued Shields for the rest of the day. Whether he was watching the Gatling gun crew at their drill, taking inventory in the supply room, or making out the ration orders for the next month, her face floated before him. Sometimes he attempted to replace Sasha's face with Susan's.

He would try to remember Susan, not as the young woman who was repelled by the conditions at Fort Verde, but as the beautiful young lady who had clung to his arm so enticingly during their Sunday afternoon strolls at West Point. How important she was to him then . . . an island of tranquility in the sea of frenzied activity that was the life of a fourth class cadet. And yet, when he tried to think of her now, the images would quiver and fade, as if made of smoke, then drift away to be replaced by the face of Sasha Quiet Stream.

Shields found more work to do in the supply room and kept himself occupied until quite late. Finally, when all the oil in the lamp had been consumed and the lamp had burned out, he decided to quit rather than refill it. He walked outside.

Under the full moon the Verde River was a stream of molten silver, wending its way beneath the peaks and mesas and through the valley outside the post. In the moonlight Fort Verde was a painting in soft shades of silver and black. Only the commandant's house, Captain Ross's quarters, escaped the unifying brush of evening. It glistened a brilliant white, its cupolas, turrets, and bay windows sprouting from the house like blooms from a rosebush. The house was obscenely large for a man to live in all alone. Shields did not want such quarters for himself.

In the middle of the quadrangle was a flag pole, its banner struck for the night, and below that a twelve-pound signal cannon, its barrel gleaming softly in the moonlight. There, leaning against the cannon, Shields saw Kevin O'Braugh, quietly smoking a pipe.

Shields strolled over to him. "Good evening, Sergeant Major."

"Lieutenant."

"Sergeant Major, can I get off the train again?" Shields asked.

"Beg pardon, sir?" O'Braugh turned to look at him, surprise clearly written on his face.

Shields laughed lightly and shook his head. "From the moment I got off the train in Prescott, I've been behaving like a jackass. I would like to start all over."

"'Tisn't all your fault, Lieutenant." O'Braugh drew thoughtfully on his pipe; then, choosing his words carefully, he went on. "I've been a bit pushy myself, tryin' to make you over into your father, when truth to tell, you're a pretty good man in your own right. You've no need of livin' in your father's shadow."

"Would you tell me a little about him?" Shields asked slowly.

"You want me to tell you about your father?" O'Braugh asked. He gave Shields a long look.

"Yes. I've always made a point of stopping people when they started holding him up to me. But I'd like to hear about him from somone who knew him, not as a hero, but as a person."

O'Braugh told Shields about his father. Some of the stories were humorous, some thrilling, but all told in such a way as to leave no doubt about what O'Braugh thought of the man.

"Now, sir, you know the story of his bravery at Gettysburg," O'Braugh continued. "So there's no need to tell you of that. But with your permission, I'd like to share another story with you . . . a personal story that perhaps will explain why I feel about the man the way I do." O'Braugh paused and took a few thoughtful puffs on his pipe.

"Yes, please do," Shields encouraged him.

"I'm Irish, you know," O'Braugh started.

Shields laughed easily. "I wouldn't have guessed."

"Aye, I guess the brogue does show me up like a sign hangin' about my neck. 'Tis no shame I have at bein' Irish you understand, but there are those who'd put us down for bein' born on the old sod. I, uh, had a particular reason for comin' to America, more'n the lookin' for my fortune, you might say."

"Did you now?"

"Aye, sir. The story begins with a puffed-up toad of a man who was high sheriff for the County Meath. He took it in his head that he was the man for my sister, managin' to forget that he already had one wife and him not livin' with her. I guess he figured that would be enough for my sister, though, of course, it wasn't, for she wanted no part of him. He pressed his attentions on her, nevertheless, and when that did no good, he began to get mean. He destroyed the tax receipts showin' my mother had already paid for the two acres of homestead she and my sister lived on. He made her pay again, and then again. Finally, he told my sister that if she couldn't find him to her likin', he'd put our dear old mother in jail.

"Mind, now, I was away in Dublin at the time an' knew nothin' of all this, for my mother and sister wanted to spare me the unpleasantness. At any rate, my sister refused the high sheriff, and my mother and sister were thrown out of their house and forced to move in with a cousin. Not satisfied with that, the sheriff called upon her again, and this time he . . ."

O'Braugh stopped for a moment and took a few puffs of his pipe, as if drawing from it the strength to go on. "He forced himself on her. My sister was so disgraced that the poor girl took her own life. I found out about it and paid the high sheriff a visit. 'Twas not my intention to do any more than bruise him up a bit and then turn him over to the law. But in the course of bruisin' him up, I hit him too hard and broke his neck. That made me the murderer of the high sheriff. I had no choice then, lad. I had to run. So I left Ireland and came to America. The war was goin' on then, and the army was full of Irish lads like myself, so it seemed the place to go."

"And that's when you met my father?"

"Aye. 'Twas another Irishman in the same regiment, big, like me, from County Meath, and also like me with no one in America to call his own. We became close friends. His name was Kevin O'Braugh."

"His name was Kevin O'Braugh?" Shields asked, frowning. "But, I don't understand. . . ."

O'Braugh held his hand up, as if telling Shields that he was about to explain. "The two of us, Timothy O'Conner and Kevin O'Braugh, were always together. Then Kevin caught a rebel bullet in his heart and died in my arms. It happened at a little town called Millerville. It wasn't even a battle you understand . . . just what they call a skirmish, not even mentioned in the history books. But my friend, Kevin, died there. That same evenin', before Kevin was put in the ground, the army sent a message to colonel Shields. The message was from the government in Ireland, askin' to extradite Timothy O'Conner for the murder of the high sheriff of County Meath. Himself, the colonel, showed me the letter, and I told him the story. I thanked him for listenin' to my side; then I held out my hands so he could put me in shackles. And then . . . I'll never forget what your father said." O'Braugh paused for a long moment.

"What did he say?" Shields asked softly.

"He said, 'Kevin O'Braugh, how are you goin' to fold the flag over the coffin of your friend, Timothy O'Conner, if your hands are shackled?' It was then that I knew what he was goin' to do."

"He sent word back that Timothy O'Conner was killed," Shields blurted.

"Aye. And I became Kevin O'Braugh, a name I've been proud to use. And when it came to me that I was to receive the Medal of Honor, General Grant pinned it to my blouse, callin' me Kevin O'Braugh all the while. I felt good about that. I felt like I was acceptin' the medal for all of us—for Kevin, for your father, and for me."

"Didn't anyone figure out what happened?" Shields asked.

"No, sir. What with the movin' about from company to company, and so many gettin' killed in the war, and the fact that both Kevin and me was new to America and had no kith or kin in this country, why, nobody ever realized the difference. Only your father knew my secret . . . and now, only you."

"Does Emily know?" Shields asked softly.

"No," O'Braugh said. He was silent for a moment. "And therein, lad, is the rub. You see, I have deep feelin's about that lady, but I dare not give voice to them, for fear of what she might think if she knew the man she knows as Kevin O'Braugh was actually Timothy O'Conner, murderer."

"Kevin," Shields said quietly, using his first name for the first time. "Don't you realize, you are the man she knows? And whatever you are, you are not a murderer. On the contrary, you are one of the finest men it has ever been my privilege to meet."

"Bless you, lad, bless you," O'Braugh said.

Out of the deep shadows and onto the moonlit parade ground, a solitary figure strode toward them. It was the company bugler, who was carrying his instrument out to the mounted megaphone to blow taps.

"Good evening, Lieutenant, Sergeant Major," the young trumpeter said softly. Shields and O'Braugh returned the soldier's greeting and then stood quietly as he raised the horn to his lips. He blew air through it a couple of times and then began to play taps. The mournful notes filled the air, rolling out across the flat, open quadrangle, hitting the hills beyond the walls of the fort, then bouncing back a second later as an even more haunting echo. Of all the military rituals, the playing of taps was the one that most affected Shields, and he never heard it without feeling a slight chill.

As the last note hung in the air for a long, sorrowful moment, Shields thought of the things he had learned today. He had learned of the love a woman could have for a father, even though he was not her real father. And he had seen the loyalty of someone like Kevin O'Braugh, a loyalty that survived even the grave.

"Corporal of the Guard, post number six and all is well!" The plaintive call from the farthest guard came drifting across the post.

"Corporal of the Guard, post number five and all is well!"

The second call was a little closer, and the calls continued down the line until post number two responded, and that call was so close that Shields felt a moment of embarrassment, as if he had intruded upon the quiet, lonely moments that were part of a sentry's privilege and duty.

"Good night, Sergeant Major," Shields said quietly.

"Good night, Lieutenant," O'Braugh replied.

Shields walked across the quadrangle to his quarters. Tonight, he had truly found a friend.

Chapter Eight

Sergeant McCorkle had tipped his chair back against the wall of the sutler's store as he read the latest copy of *Harper's Weekly*. He was supposed to be supervising the morning stables, but he had a corporal overseeing the work detail while he rested in the shade of the sutler's store front porch.

"Ha!" he said to Branson. "Listen to this, from 'Humors of the Day.' A man went into a bank with a forty-year-old wife. 'I wish to turn her in,' he says to the cashier. 'Why, I don't understand, sir,' the cashier replies. 'Turn her in for what?' 'Why, I wish to turn her in for two twenty-year-old women, like changing a bill,' the man answers." McCorkle laughed loudly. "Did you get that, Branson? Turn her in for two twenty-year-olds."

"Yes," Branson said. "I got it." Branson was standing on the front porch, drinking a cup of coffee and looking out toward the signal cannon. There he saw Sasha posing for a portrait with Lieutenant Shields. He also saw Dr. Hartfield going into the barracks for morning sick call, so he knew that Chief Chatoma would be alone in the hospital. The men who had been wounded during the stagecoach fight had all been released, so that meant Chatoma was for the moment the only patient there.

Branson tossed the rest of his coffee out on the ground in front of the porch. "Watch things for me, will you, Sergeant McCorkle? I have some business to tend to."

"Sure," McCorkle said, not looking up from his paper.

Branson set his cup on the porch railing and then walked over to the hospital. Inside, he found only one orderly on duty. The man was busy cleaning instruments, and he looked up when Branson came in.

"What can I do for you, Mr. Branson?"

"I just want to check on the old chief, that's all," Branson said lightly.

"Sure. He was awake a few minutes ago," the orderly said, smiling. "Go on down and talk to him." He turned away from Branson and went on with his work.

Branson walked between the two rows of empty beds until he reached the last bed, where Chatoma was sitting propped up on two pillows, looking through the window.

"Hello, Chatoma," Branson said cheerfully.

Chatoma looked around, but he did not speak. Instead he nodded and then looked steadily at Branson with deep brown, unfathomable eyes.

"How do you feel?"

"I feel better today," Chatoma said simply.

"Good, good," Branson replied. "Because you and I have some business to talk about."

"Business?" Chatoma's eyes narrowed.

"Yes. Business that I think you will like." Branson smiled broadly. "Chief, I'm prepared to put a lot of money in your hands."

"I do not need money," Chatoma said, slowly shaking his head.

"Sure you do. Everyone can use a little more money," Branson coaxed.

"How can I use money? Does the river need money for fish? Do the mountains need money for deer? Does the forest need money for berries and nuts? I would not know what to do with money."

Branson chuckled. "Don't worry about that, Chief. Once you get it, you'll know what to do with it, all right. And all you have to do for it is give me title to the land grants your tribe holds between Prescott and Sedona. Hell, you aren't even living there. You'll never miss it."

"No," Chatoma said firmly. "We have spoken of this before. I cannot sell the land of my people."

"Sure you can. You're the chief. If you sign the deed, it'll hold up in court, I promise you."

"I will not sell," Chatoma said, and his deep brown eyes fixed Branson with an icy stare.

"I'm prepared to offer twice as much as I offered before," he wheedled.

"I will not sell," Chatoma said angrily.

"Damn it, man!" Branson hissed. "What are you trying to do? Hold me up for more money?"

"How much money is there in the world?"

"How much? I don't know. Why would you ask? That is a dumb question," Branson replied impatiently.

"If you had all the money there is in the world, I still would not sell the land to you," Chatoma said coldly.

"Listen, old man! You're dying! Don't you know that? You're dying! And believe me, after you're dead the army is going to run your people off the land anyway. There will be nothing left for them, do you understand me? Nothing! If you sell to me now, at least they'll have something."

"No!" Chatoma said. "Go now." His voice grew louder, and his face darkened with rage.

"I'm not going anywhere until we talk this out," Branson bellowed at him.

"Go!" Chatoma demanded angrily. He raised up in his bed and pointed toward the door. "Go now!" he shouted. Chatoma began coughing violently, a deep, racking cough. For a long moment he could not catch his breath, and he grabbed his chest. The orderly, having heard the loud voices, came running down to see what was going on.

"What is it?" he said anxiously. "What's wrong with Chatoma?"

"You!" Chatoma said, gasping and pointing at Branson. "You go now!"

"Mr. Branson, sir, I don't know what this is all about," the orderly said nervously. "But maybe you'd better go now and come back when the doctor is here."

"That old Indian is crazy," Branson fumed, and he stormed out the back door.

"Mark," Sasha called. He turned to see her walking quickly across the ground to the signal cannon against which he was leaning. Her voice was frightened and angry, and Shields wondered what was wrong. When she had left him only a few moments earlier to see how her father was getting along, she had been happy and relaxed. Now she was back, and she was obviously very upset and agitated.

"What is it, Sasha? What's wrong?"

"I would like you to tell Mr. Branson not to see my father anymore," she said firmly.

"I don't understand. Why would Branson want to see your father? And why would your father object if he did call on him?"

Sasha told him what her father had said of Branson's visit, of his hounding him about the land.

"All right, I'll speak with Branson about it," Shields promised.

When Shields confronted the man with it, Branson laughed easily. "Well, there you go," he said. "That's just an example of the difference between a red man and a white man. I was just trying to be neighborly, but that old coot would have no part of it. Tell you the truth, Lieutenant, I don't think Chatoma even knows what he's talking about."

"Perhaps not," Shields agreed. "But according to his daughter, he was very upset by your visit. Did you attempt to force him into selling his land?"

"Force him to sell his land? Do you think you could force Chatoma to do anything he didn't want to do? No, I didn't try to force him. I admit, I did make an offer to buy the land grants, but I was really just relaying a message to him from Connell and Trapman. You remember them, don't you? They were the businessmen who were caught up in that stagecoach raid the other day. Anyway, they showed some interest in buying land out here as investment property. They seemed particularly interested in land between Prescott and Sedona. I told them that land belonged to the Indians, and they asked me to make an offer, so I did. I thought it might be to the old man's advantage to sell, that's all. I had no idea he would act like that."

"That's funny," Shields mused.

"What's funny?"

"That they would be particularly interested in land between Prescott and Sedona. That's where they were attacked.

And from the way they were acting, all they wanted to do was to get away from here as fast as they could."

"I guess after the fear passed, they realized the potential of this area," Branson explained smoothly. He smiled broadly. "I have to admit, I helped sell them on it. After all, I have great faith in the future of this country . . . and in the army to keep it safe."

"Yes, well, I'm sure your faith is justified. In the meantime, I have to ask you to leave the chief alone."

"You have my word on that, Lieutenant. I won't bother him again."

Branson was true to his word, and for the next several days he stayed away from Chatoma. Chatoma appeared to be getting better, though his progress was fairly slow, which meant both he and his daughter became extended guests of the post.

Shields saw Sasha everywhere, riding outside the walls, walking across the parade ground, talking with the other women of the post. But the opportunity for him to be alone with her never presented itself, and he made no effort to seek it out. Twice during the next several days, he took long patrols out to look for Manitoro, once staying away from the post for four days. He did not encounter Manitoro on either patrol.

It was two weeks later that Emily, pulling the coach to a sliding halt in front of the headquarters building, presented Shields with a letter from Susan Hamilton. The return address showed that she was now back in Washington. Shields took the letter without a word and then went off to be by himself while he read it.

"What do you think's in the letter?" Emily asked O'Braugh as they watched Shields walk away.

O'Braugh chuckled. "Only a woman would be so nosy as to inquire."

"Oh, so it's nosy I am, is it?" Emily protested. "And I suppose all the gossip of the town I share with you isn't a sign of your bein' nosy?"

"A thirst for news and nothing more," O'Braugh answered. A smile twitched at his lips. "I harbor no curiosity about another person's mail."

"Nor I," Emily said. "Except for worryin' that the young lieutenant will be for goin' back to Washington soon."

"If you're a bettin' woman, Emily, bet that he'll stay here, regardless of what the letter says to him."

"Do you really think so?"

"Aye. The lad is greatly changed."

As he sat down alone in the shade of a wagon to read the letter, Shields could smell the perfume that Susan had put on the page before putting it in the envelope. When he had received such letters at West Point, the perfume had worked its way with him. Here, under the great open sky of the West, it seemed a rather foolish affectation.

My Dearest Mark,

I hope and pray that you are over any hurt I may have caused you by my sudden and unexpected departure from Fort Verde. But really, dearest, you must understand. When I saw the perfectly horrendous way we were expected to live, and those awful fishwives who were to be my only social contact, well, I just couldn't put up with that.

Already, several parties have been given here in Washington. And as you might expect, my social position is such that I have my choice as to which parties I can attend. I flatter myself by thinking that invitations are so readily extended to me because I enhance any party I attend, merely by being a guest. Therefore I have, of course, chosen only the most acceptable affairs, leaving the poor imitators wanting for lack of my company.

Colonel William Godfrey inquired of you yesterday. You can appreciate that it would be totally unacceptable to attend a party alone, so Colonel Godfrey graciously extended an offer to be my escort at yesterday's affair. We had a fine time, and I teased him about his newly grown beard. You should have seen how funny he was. Sometimes I think men are but children, and the more handsome or important they are, the more childish they become.

You, of course, are the exception, for despite the

fact that you are the most handsome man I have ever met, you are also the most stable and dedicated. Everyone has inquired about you, and I have told them that you are now in the West, but will soon return to assume a position of much importance. Incidentally, I gave your letter to my father, and he has agreed that you shall be on his staff. Can you believe he actually suggested that you should fulfill this assignment first? I soon talked him out of that, you can believe. There is one thing more you must do, however. Father says you must submit a formal application for transfer through channels. When it reaches Washington, he will see to it that it is approved.

I attended the Eucharist Service at the National Cathedral on Sunday. How beautiful the Cathedral is with the magnificent reredos, the elegant hangings and marble altar, the lovely organ and choir, creating music that sounds as if it comes from heaven itself. What a magnificent place to have our wedding! Then, when I think of that horrible little chapel at Fort Verde, and the awful way those pathetic women were decorating it . . . as if I would be satisfied with their ridiculous wild branches and wilted wildflowers, I want to laugh.

Mark, again let me tell you how sorry I am if I hurt you by leaving. However, I'm sure that by now you have had time to think things over, and you agree that I did the right thing. Hurry back, dearest. Hurry back to Washington where we both belong.

With the greatest affection, I remain,

Your Susan

After Shields had finished reading the letter, he looked at it for a long moment. The Washington scene, and Susan, seemed very remote to him now. It was not just a matter of distance. By train, the distance could be covered in less than a week. It was something else, a remoteness that could never be bridged.

Shields put the letter aside, then picked up his sketch pad. He was drawing still another picture of Sasha, but she had not posed for this one. He was drawing this one from memory—the image he retained of her when he had first seen her at the head of the group of Indians at the Webb ranch.

"You can draw pictures of me without me sitting still for you?" Sasha said softly.

Shields jumped, surprised at the sound of her voice. She had walked up on him so quietly that he had not heard her. He smiled and handed the pad to her.

"If you lived with the Indians, you would be a medicine man," Sasha said, admiring the sketch with a delighted smile. "You have great medicine in your hands."

"Medicine? I can't heal people," Shields protested.

Sasha laughed. "To say you have medicine does not mean you are a doctor. Medicine means power. People who have great medicine are very respected by the Indians."

"And do you have great medicine?" Shields asked.

Sasha untied her hair and then shook it and let it cascade down across her shoulders. It framed her head in glittering gold, and she laughed. "My hair is my medicine," she said. "The Indians say I have captured the sun."

"I'd say that's a pretty good way of expressing it," Shields agreed. "Do you like living with the Indians?"

"Yes, I think so. I can't remember anything else."

"You don't remember your parents?" Shields asked sadly.

"Barely. I remember my mother . . . she smelled good, like flowers. I remember my father's face; it was rough when he hugged me . . . not a bad rough, a good rough." She put her hand to Shields's cheek and rubbed it softly, feeling the beginning stubble of his beard, grown since that morning. "Your face is rough like his. Indians aren't like that."

"Indians don't have beards," Shields explained. He rubbed his jaw and smiled. "Sometimes I think they're lucky."

"You have a letter from your woman," Sasha said, suddenly changing the subject.

"What?"

"Emily told me you have a letter from your woman. I saw her when she was here. She is very beautiful."

"Yes."

"Emily says you might leave. You might go back to be with your woman."

Shields looked at her. Her clear blue eyes in her guileless face gazed at him. In those simple statements she had clearly outlined his dilemma. Now that he was confronted with it, he realized for the first time that he would have to make a decision about Susan once and for all. He sighed and shook his head.

"No," he finally said. "No, I'm not going back to Washington, and I'm not going back to Susan. I thought I loved her, but she was a part of me that doesn't exist anymore. I don't know whether I'm going to stay in the army or not . . . but I know I'm not going to leave Fort Verde for a while. I'm not putting in for a transfer."

Sasha smiled broadly. "You mean she is not your woman anymore?"

"She is not my woman anymore," Shields said, shaking his head.

"That is good," Sasha said enthusiastically. "That means I can be your woman!"

Shields was so surprised by her outburst that he just stared at her for a moment.

"Do you not want me for your woman?" she asked, unable to understand why he had not answered.

"Sasha, it isn't as simple as all that," Shields began, trying to explain, but before he could finish, Sasha turned and walked away from him, her face a mask of grief. "Sasha," he called after her. "Sasha, wait."

Sasha wondered why he spurned her offer. She knew he thought she was beautiful; he had told her so. And he would not draw pictures of her if he did not really mean that. So why did he not want her to be his woman? Was it because she was an Indian?

No, that could not be it, because she was not really an Indian. She was white, just as he was. But she dressed as an Indian. That was it! If she would dress as a white woman, then she could be his woman!

Sasha had seen dresses for sale in the sutler's store, and she decided she would immediately go and look at them again. She was buoyant as she hurried across the post and skipped lightly into the store.

"Hello, miss," one of Branson's clerks said when he saw

her holding the sleeve of one of the dresses in her hand, carefully examining it. "I see you're looking at that red dress. It sure would be pretty on you."

"Oh, do you think so?" Sasha asked.

"Absolutely. That dress was made for you."

Sasha's eyes grew wide. "Really? This dress was made for me? But how did the person who made it know I would want it?"

The clerk had not expected her to take his answer so literally, and he did not know how to answer, so he let her response slide by. Instead, he asked, "Would you like to buy that dress?"

"Yes, please," Sasha replied.

"That will be a dollar twenty-five," the clerk said.

"Is that a lot of money?"

"How much do you have?"

"I have no money."

"You have no money?" the clerk asked in an exasperated tone of voice. He snatched the dress from her hands and hung it back on the rack. "Then how do you expect to buy this dress?"

"But . . . I don't understand. You said it was made for me," she protested, puzzled and confused.

"And so it was," Branson said soothingly, suddenly coming around from behind the counter.

"Mr. Branson, she has no money," the clerk whispered hoarsely to him.

"That's quite all right, Dobson." Branson took the dress off the rack again and handed it to Sasha. "It's yours, Sasha. I make a present of it to you."

"Thank you," Sasha said, delighted. She gratefully took the dress from Branson and ran happily from the store.

"Mr. Branson, I don't understand," the clerk said.

"It's very simple," Branson said smoothly. "Her father has something I want. If I give her the dress, he may be more disposed toward giving me what I want. It's called baiting the calf to get the bull."

Before Sasha put on her dress, she walked over to the hospital to speak with her father. He smiled happily when she came to see him.

"You are a good daughter to come to me when I am sick," Chatoma said, taking her hands in his.

"And why not?" Sasha replied. "When I was a little girl, did you not come to me when I was sick?"

"Yes," Chatoma said. "When we first got you, you were sick many times. I thought all white girls were sick many times. Then you became more Indian than white, and you grew strong and healthy."

Blushing, Sasha looked away quickly. Since her encounter with Shields, she had been wishing she was more white than Indian. Now she was ashamed that she had had such thoughts, and she could not look her father in the eye.

"Daughter, what is it?" Chatoma asked, seeing the confusion in her eyes and knowing her so well.

"It is nothing," she said much too quickly.

"You say it is nothing with your lips," Chatoma said softly. "But with your eyes and with your heart, I see that you are troubled."

Sasha looked at Chatoma. No biological daughter could have been more open and dependent upon a father's love and wisdom than she was at that moment. "Father, am I Indian, or am I white?"

An expression of sadness came over Chatoma's face. This was a question he knew would be asked someday. It was inevitable, but though he knew it would come, he had not looked forward to it. He sighed. "Tell me, daughter. Why do you ask this now?"

"I . . . I have a reason," Sasha stammered, trying to reveal her thoughts.

"I think I know the reason. It is the young soldier-chief."

"If I am an Indian, I cannot be his woman," Sasha blurted. "But since I am white, I cannot be the woman of an Indian. If I am not Indian and I am not white, I am nothing."

"Why do you think this? Has someone told you this?"

"No. But some things are not meant to be," she said sadly.

"You think you are so wise, but you are so young. Maybe there are things you think you know, but do not know."

"I know this," Sasha said earnestly. "A bird and a fish might fall in love. But if they get married, where will they live?"

"And you think you are a bird and the young soldier-chief is a fish?" His brown eyes began to twinkle.

"Yes." Sasha nodded her head mournfully.

Chatoma laughed. "Then listen to this. There are birds that can swim, and there are fish that can fly. Why is this so, if Usen does not let birds and fish marry?"

Sasha looked at Chatoma in surprise. "What are you telling me, Father?"

"I am telling you to look in here," he said, putting his hand over his heart. "Not here." He put his hand on his skin. "What is to be, will be. If you are to be the woman of the young soldier-chief . . ."

"His name is Mark," Sasha said quickly.

Chatoma patted Sasha's hand affectionately. "If you are to be Mark's woman, you will be."

"And you will not make him give you too many gifts for me? You will not frighten him away?"

"My lodge will be open to him," Chatoma said, an understanding smile warming his deep brown eyes.

With her eyes shining brightly, Sasha stood up quickly. "I am going to him now," she said. She smiled. "I am going to show him that I, too, can be a fish."

Shields was still sitting in the same place, still working on Sasha's portrait, when he saw her walking toward him. She was wearing a red dress, and though she was beautiful in it, she looked a little awkward about it. She moved stiffly, as if uncomfortable with all the material. She stopped just in front of him and smiled sheepishly.

"You do not have to tell me why you did not want me as your woman before," Sasha said.

"Sasha, I—"

She held up her hand and stopped him. "No," she said. "Then I was Sasha. Now I am Lily. You see, I am Lily Mason, white woman. I am white; you are white. I can be your woman."

Shields did not know what to say. He did not want to hurt her feelings again, and yet she was wearing her heart on her sleeve, so innocently open that she could be hurt by the slightest word. He knew he would have to be careful.

"Where did you get the dress?" he asked.

"Mr. Branson gave it to me."

"He gave it to you? You didn't buy it?" he asked with a frown.

"I could not buy it. I have no money," she said simply.

"Does Branson know you have no money?"

"Yes. I told him this. Do you think it is beautiful?" she asked eagerly.

"Yes, it's very beautiful."

Sasha smiled broadly. "It was made for me," she said. "He told me so."

"Sasha . . ."

"Lily."

"Lily, you shouldn't have taken it."

Sasha frowned. "Why not? You said yourself it is beautiful."

"Yes, but you did not pay for it."

"Mr. Branson said I did not have to. He said it was made for me, and he gave it to me."

Shields ran his hand through his hair and sighed in exasperation. "Don't you understand? He is going to expect something in return. People don't just give you things for no reason. I wish you would take it back."

"You don't like it," she said, disappointed.

"That's not the point." He sighed deeply.

Sasha's eyes welled with tears, and she looked at him with an expression that showed the depth of the pain she was feeling over his rejection. Slowly, despondently, she turned and walked away from him.

Shields watched her go, wondering what he could do to correct the situation. He knew he had hurt her again, and that was the last thing he wanted to do. Suddenly he realized that what he was feeling for this woman was more than mere sympathy for her plight. *Can it be?* he wondered. *Can it be that I am in love with her?*

Chapter Nine

Manitoro walked over to the rock overhang and looked down into the valley twenty-five hundred feet below. There, just coming off the valley floor and starting up the winding mountain road, was the stage. From this vantage point it was so tiny that it looked like a toy stage and team. He could remember a toy stage and team from somewhere, although the misty recollection was so distant that it seemed to belong to someone else.

Manitoro and half a dozen warriors were waiting for the stage at the turnout just below the crest. It would be a long, exhausting climb for the team, and Manitoro knew that the driver would halt the horses at the turnout to let the animals rest, to check the brakes before the descent down the other side, and to allow the passengers time to "stretch their legs," a gentle euphemism for walking into the woods to relieve themselves.

It was because they would be stopping that Manitoro had chosen this place to wait. It made the attack much easier and, as he had learned, the secret to being a leader was to guarantee the success of his battles. Even the location of this attack was a guarantee of success, because it was taking place between Flagstaff and Sedona. So far there had been no attacks in this area, and Manitoro knew that the driver, guard, and passengers would not be expecting trouble here. Manitoro turned and walked back to his men, satisfied with the choices he had made.

When he knew by the movement of the sun that the

stage had been climbing for nearly an hour, Manitoro returned to the overhang to see how close the stage was. He stretched out on a rock and looked down to see that it had turned onto one of the switchbacks. By now the coach was close enough for him to see that the woman who frequently drove was not driving this time. This stage was being driven by an old man with white hair and a long, white beard. Sitting alongside the driver, holding the shotgun across his lap, was the guard. He was much younger than the driver.

Manitoro scrambled back to the others and signaled for them to get ready, keep quiet, and stay out of sight. He did not want anything to happen that would expose their position and deprive them of the element of surprise. The coach would be here in just a few moments; then they could strike.

As the seconds passed, the sounds made by the approaching coach grew louder. Manitoro could hear the pop of the whip and the creak of the stage as it rocked in its thoroughbraces, as well as the snorting and puffing of the horses as they strained in the harness. He rose up and peered over the edge of the rock just as the driver hauled back on the reins.

"Whoa, hold it up there, team," the driver shouted. The stage rumbled to a halt, and the horses stood still, breathing loudly.

"They do not see us," one of Manitoro's men said quietly, and Manitoro held his hand out in a signal to be silent.

"Folks," the driver called down to his passengers, "we gotta let these here animals get their wind back before we start down the other side. They's a real purty view from up here, so why'n't you take a break and stretch your legs out a mite?"

Two people left the stage. One man was obviously a farmer, big and rawboned. The other was small and mousy. Manitoro looked over at his warriors. Four were armed with rifles, two with bow and arrows. All were aiming and ready for his signal. He brought his hand down sharply.

The driver and the shotgun guard went down in the first volley. The farmer let out a curse and then ran to the shotgun guard and picked up his gun. Manitoro admired the man's courage, but it was futile. The farmer fired toward the Indians, but he was shooting a shotgun, and Manitoro and his warriors were beyond the range of such a weapon. The spent buckshot rattled harmlessly off the rocks. The Indians returned fire, and this time the farmer and the other passenger went down.

One of the warriors shot a fire arrow into the stage, and it started burning. The others fired their rifles at the stage, and Manitoro could see splinters of wood flying as the bullets poked holes through the side. A second fire arrow, then a third was shot into the stage, and soon the coach was a roaring inferno.

Manitoro could see that all four victims were dead and no return fire was coming from the coach. The horses stamped around nervously, but they were well trained to the harness, so they stood still, even though the coach was burning behind them. Manitoro held up his hand to order his warriors to cease fire. Everyone was dead; there was no need to waste any more bullets.

"Get the horses," Manitoro commanded, and the warriors scrambled over the rocks and then ran down to claim the spoils of their victory.

One of the Indians hurried over to the burning coach and looked inside. "Aiyee," he shouted.

"What is it?" Manitoro asked.

The warrior opened the door and pulled out two small forms. "Children. A boy and girl," he said, laying the children out on the ground alongside the others. Manitoro saw that both of them were dead, hit by the rifle fire that had been aimed at the coach. No one had known they were inside. They had obviously been lying on the floor, trying to hide, but it had done them no good.

Manitoro stared at the children for a long moment. Would he have killed them if he had known about them? Perhaps. Or perhaps he would have taken them. It did not matter now. What was done was done. He had a sense of having been here before, and unconsciously he fingered the amulet that hung around his neck. The thought was disquieting, and he turned away from the bodies. He could do nothing to change things now. "Get the horses," he ordered gruffly. "The smoke will bring others."

The warriors cut the horses from the harness and led them off. Then, jumping on their own animals, they rode away, whooping triumphantly. Behind them the pillar of smoke rose hundreds of feet in the air, marking the spot of their atrocity.

"The heathens! The savages! They murdered the children! They murdered the children!"

The horse galloped down the main street of Sedona, its rider yelling at the top of his voice. Emily was in her office at the head of the street, and when she heard the commotion, she got up from her desk and went to the door to see what was going on.

The rider had attracted not only Emily's attention, but that of the entire town, and people were streaming out of saloons, stores, restaurants, and hotels to follow him down the street. One man had been in the barbershop getting a shave, and he hurried down the boardwalk, the apron still tied around him, his face half covered with lather, while the barber, waving his razor overhead, ran along behind.

The rider reined in his horse in front of the stage office and looked down at Emily. His face was flushed, his eyes wide with excitement. His horse breathed hard, and Emily could see the animal lathering heavily from its exertion. The townspeople began to crowd around her as she spoke to the frantic man.

"Mr. Simpson, what is it?" Emily asked. "What are you getting everyone so worked up about?"

"It's your stage, Miz Rourke," Simpson said, getting down from his horse. He removed his canteen from the pommel and took a swallow of water before he went on.

"What about my stage?" Emily demanded.

Simpson pulled the canteen down and wiped his mouth with the back of his hand. "It's sittin' up at Milo Pass. That is, what's left of it. It's done been burnt down to charcoal."

"What?" Emily exclaimed.

"Indians, Miz Rourke. It was Indians that done it."

"Indians?" Emily gasped. "What about Davey, my driver? And Charley, the shotgun?"

"Dead," Simpson said. "And all the passengers, too."

Emily felt a sinking sensation in the pit of her stomach. "All? Mr. Simpson, the McAlister children were supposed to be on that stage. They'd been visiting their grandparents up in Flagstaff."

Simpson swallowed hard and looked at the ground. "Them,

too," he said. "They're layin' out on the ground alongside the other two . . . some farmer I don't know and Carter Hanks."

"Carter Hanks? The bank teller?"

Simpson nodded.

"Why, he's my son's Sunday school teacher," someone in the crowd said. "You couldn't meet a better fella than him."

"And the McAlister young 'uns. Why, you've seen 'em, ain't you? Playin' aroun' down by the well."

"Them murderin' redskins," someone said angrily.

"I don't understand," Emily said, closing her eyes as if to block out the terrible news. "We've never had Indian trouble up there. That's way off Manitoro's normal path."

"Maybe we ain't had before," Simpson said. "But we sure got it now. They was arrows all over the place."

"What did you do with the bodies?"

"Do? Why, I didn't do nothin' with 'em," Simpson said. "The coach was still smolderin'. Could be them heathens was still hangin' aroun', just waitin' to see who else they could get."

"We can't just leave 'em up there," a townsman chimed in. "Miz Rourke, it's your driver. You don't want to just leave 'em up there, do you?"

"No, of course not," Emily said. She ran her hand through her hair and desperately scanned the anguished and angry faces surrounding her. Then she noticed Jerome Baker in the crowd. Baker owned a freight line. "Jerome, I'll pay the fee if you'll take a wagon up for them."

"I'll go," Baker said, with a nod. "But I ain't goin' alone. I got to have some men go with me."

"I'll go," one of the crowd said. "And I'll get half a dozen of my friends to go with me."

"I'll go, too," another volunteered, and within moments, an impromptu force of fifteen men had presented themselves.

"All right, men, meet me down at the stable," Baker said. "I'd like to get up there and back before it gets dark."

Numb with shock and grief, Emily watched them leave. Then she slowly walked back into her office and sat down at her desk and thought sadly of Davey Potter. Davey had come to work for them when her husband had left the army to start the stage business. He was an old hand at driving coaches. And now he was dead . . . and Charley. And the McAlister children. Emily sighed and hid her face in her hands. She would have to break the news to Mr. and Mrs. McAlister when they came to pick up the children. What a dreadful task that would be.

It did not take long for the McAlisters to find out. News traveled fast, and when there was a tragedy involved, it traveled even faster. The McAlisters came roaring up to the office less than half an hour later, Sam driving the buckboard, Rose holding her hands over her face. Sam, ashen-faced, climbed down and started toward the office, but Emily hurried to meet him outside.

"I'm so sorry," Emily said. It broke her heart to have to tell them, though it was obvious that they already knew.

"Then . . . it's . . . true?" Sam asked in a quiet, strained voice.

"Yes," Emily said softly.

"Oh, God!" Rose McAlister wailed, and Sam hurried over to put his arms around her. Emily watched them through tear-dimmed eyes, wishing with all that was in her that she did not have to substantiate the terrible news.

Sam was quiet for a moment, and then he looked at Emily. Though he was not sobbing aloud, his eyes were red-rimmed, and tears were streaming down his cheeks. "You should have done something!" he shouted.

"What?" Emily was shocked at his sudden outburst.

"You were responsible for them," he went on. "We entrusted them to your care and you . . . you let this happen!"

"Mr. McAlister," Emily said desperately. "Please, I can't tell you how sorry I am . . . how my heart aches for you. But you can't possibly think I could have done anything to prevent it."

"They were your responsibility!" he said again.

"Sam!" Rose McAlister sobbed. "Please, you know it wasn't her fault."

Sam held his wife close for a moment longer. Then he looked back at Emily. The anger in his face was gone now, replaced by a pain as intense as any Emily had ever seen.

"Please," he finally said in a quiet, choked voice. "Please forgive me. I don't know what I'm saying. I'm so . . . so . . ." He could not finish, nor could he any longer hold the sobs in check.

Emily grabbed the porch support pillar and turned away

from them, blinded by her own tears. *God, that this would happen . . . that I should have to witness it*, she thought.

The farmer's name was Sylvanus Green. His wife and two grown sons came down from Flagstaff the next day to recover his body. Emily watched them through the window. The widow, a gray-haired, stoutly built woman, sat stoically in the front of the wagon. Her two grown sons, their faces expressionless, as if unwilling to share their grief with strangers, put their father's body under a tarpaulin in the back of the wagon. Then they drove away, all the while staring straight ahead.

The bodies of Davey, Charley, Carter Hanks, and the two McAlister children were taken to Tom Welsh, Sedona's undertaker. The citizens of Sedona planned a mass funeral for that same afternoon, and though Emily did not go to look at them, she knew that all four bodies were lying in gruesome display in their highly polished caskets in the front window of Sikes's Hardware Store. Never at any time during the day were there fewer than thirty people standing outside the hardware store, looking at that tragic sight with morbid curiosity.

Although Emily did not want to, she did attend the funeral. Having one mass funeral seemed too much of an event to her, and she felt it lessened the dignity they each deserved. Undignified or not, the funeral drew every man, woman, and child in town. Only those too sick or too old to move stayed behind; more than two hundred people gathered on the hill at the cemetery to listen to the preacher.

After the funeral a delegation of citizens headed by Jerome Baker called upon Emily. She was surprised until they explained what they wanted.

"We want you to go to Fort Verde," Baker said. "You know the soldiers better than any of us. You used to be married to one."

"Yes, and since it was your coach that was burned, you got more right than any of us to request help."

"Why, I'm sure the army is already providing all the help they can," Emily said.

"No, Miz Rourke, they ain't. If they was, they'd march out to that village an' run all them Indians out . . . run 'em all the way down to San Carlos."

"Are you talking about the Tonto Apache? Chatoma's village?" Emily asked.

"Yes, we are."

"They're peaceful Indians," Emily protested.

"How do we know that?" Baker demanded. "You said yourself that this was out of Manitoro's territory. It could've been someone from Chatoma's camp. Now, we want you to go out to the fort and get us some help."

" 'Cause if the army don't do nothin', we'll go out there an' clean out the village ourselves," another threatened angrily.

Emily thought about the tension that had grown in Sedona and the desperation and anger in the faces of the men in front of her. If she took a delegation out to talk to the army, there would at least be some control over what happened. If she did nothing, the town's citizens were likely to take matters into their own hands, and there was no telling where that would lead.

"All right," she finally agreed. "Tomorrow morning have six representatives from the town here at my office. I'll take a stage out to the fort, and we'll speak with Captain Ross."

When the coach pulled to a halt in front of the headquarters building the next day, everyone at the fort knew that something was amiss. In the first place it was not a scheduled appearance for the coach, and in the second, the leading members of the town of Sedona were on board. It looked like a delegation of some sort, and Ross invited them into his office. Farley Branson, seeing them arrive, managed to have himself invited to the meeting as well.

"Well," Ross said, leaning back against his desk and looking around at the citizens of the town. "To what do I owe the honor?"

Jerome Baker looked around and then cleared his throat. "Cap'n, we're a delegation representin' the town of Sedona," he said. "We got the leadin' businessmen of the community here, all of one voice, and they've asked me to talk for 'em."

"All right, Mr. Baker," Ross said. "Please, go on."

"Well, sir, I think . . . that is, we think this business with the Indians has gone far enough."

"Yeah," one of the others added. "And we want the army to do somethin' about it."

"What exactly, Mr. Baker, did you have in mind?" Ross asked.

"We want you to get it stopped."

Ross ran his hand through his hair and then walked over to the map hanging on his wall and pointed to it. "Gentlemen, I have an area of responsibility that is as large as the states of Maryland, Delaware, and Rhode Island combined. And to police this area, I have but two troops of cavalry. Less than two hundred men. Even so, I am doing everything possible to protect the civilians in my jurisdiction. Right now Lieutenant Shields has a patrol out in pursuit of Manitoro."

"Not good enough," Branson suddenly interrupted. "We demand more."

"See here, Mr. Branson," Ross said. "I hardly think you are qualified to speak on behalf of this delegation."

"Who better than I to speak?" Branson asked. "Don't forget, sir, I, too, am a civilian. And I am a businessman, doing business not only with the U.S. Army, but with the civilians of this territory as well. And I, like these gentlemen, have suffered losses at the hands of the Indians. I told you last week that one of my wagons is missing. It has never shown up, and I fear the worst for the driver and guard, to say nothing of the hundreds of dollars' worth of merchandise that was lost to me."

"Mr. Branson, you live here on the fort with the rest of us," Ross said. "You should understand better than anyone the limits imposed upon me by orders."

"I know also, Captain Ross, that you have been given some degree of leeway in making decisions. And I know that the army rewards initiative when commanders are successful. Think, man! Think back to your time with General Terry. You do remember the scene, don't you? The vultures circling overhead, the stench of death in your nostrils, the mutilated remains of nearly two hundred of your fellow soldiers lying on the battlefield. Custer's dishonor . . . you do remember that, don't you?"

"Yes . . . yes, of course I remember," Ross said.

"Here, then, is your opportunity to redeem the army's stained honor. Trust me, Captain Ross. You show the War Department a victory over these Indians, and you will earn the respect and admiration not only of the army but of the country."

Branson's words were delivered as if he were a politician giving a speech, and when he finished, the members of the delegation applauded him. "Hear, hear," one of them said. "Never were truer words spoken."

"What about it, Captain?" Branson asked.

"All right," Ross agreed. "I will personally lead a campaign against Manitoro. And after we have him taken care of, I will remove all remaining Indians to the reservation at San Carlos. Will that satisfy you?"

"That will satisfy us," Baker said, noting that the others had nodded their approval.

Only Emily showed uneasiness with what had been said.

Chatoma wanted to leave his hospital bed to take a walk, and Dr. Hartfield thought a little fresh air and exercise would be good for him, so he agreed. Sasha went with him, and their walk took them out of the fort and up the side of a nearby hill. Sasha had packed a small lunch to take with them, and they sat on a flat rock, looking down on the fort. From this vantage point they could see everything going on, the soldiers in the stables, the troopers at drill.

It was common knowledge that Ross was about to undertake a major expedition against the Indians, and Sasha feared that the captain would make no distinction between good Indians and bad Indians. She spoke of her concern to Chatoma.

"I don't understand why he would want to punish people who have given him no trouble," she said. "It will not stop Manitoro from attacking."

"Captain Ross is a man with much ambition," Chatoma explained gently to her. "He feels he should be a much higher chief than he is, and he thinks this is a way to do that."

"He is a man of greed," Sasha said.

"Yes," Chatoma said, nodding slowly. "Manitoro is also a man of greed, but no one has yet seen it."

"Manitoro is a man of greed?"

"Yes."

"Why do you say this, father? He is an angry man . . . a man who wishes to drive the whites away, but he is not a greedy man."

"Have you not seen that every raid Manitoro has made has been on land that the sutler, Branson, has tried to buy?"

Sasha was silent for a moment. She had not thought about it before, but now that it was pointed out to her, she realized that this was true.

"What are you saying, Father?" Sasha asked.

"I do not believe this is without plan," Chatoma went on. "I believe Manitoro is doing the work of evil men not to drive the white man away, but to drive the Indian away."

Later that same afternoon, Sasha sought out Shields to share with him what Chatoma had told her. Shields listened with interest, though he was a little skeptical.

"What your father is suggesting is that Manitoro and Farley Branson have come to some accord, whereby Branson can get control of the land of your people."

"Yes."

"I can't believe that Manitoro has a mind that devious," he said. "And anyway, the question is, why would he do it? What's in it for Manitoro? He has no need for money."

"Not money," Sasha said. "But weapons, maybe."

"Weapons?" Shields looked at her in surprise.

"Yes. Where else would he get them? He already has many more guns than all the people of my father's village."

"Maybe he stole them."

"Where? He has raided only stagecoaches, way stations, and small ranches and farms. There are not many guns at such places."

"That's true," Shields agreed slowly. "But his last raid, against the stage from Flagstaff, could serve no purpose. It was off the land your father controls."

"Yes. I admit, I do not know why he would do such a thing."

"Unless," Shields went on, stroking his chin thoughtfully, "unless he did it to whip the people of Sedona into a frenzy. And if that's the case, he was certainly successful, for they have convinced Captain Ross to mount an expedition."

"You will be going on this expedition?" Sasha asked.

"Yes."

"Against my people?"

Shields put his hand out gently to touch Sasha. He did not realize, until that moment, that this was the first physical contact between them. He felt something almost tangible leap through his fingers, and he was surprised that he could feel so much for this girl. He turned and gazed into her clear blue eyes.

"I promise, Sasha, I will bring no harm to your people," he said firmly.

Sasha stared at him, her eyes open so wide that, again, he could see into her very soul. He saw innocence, trust, and unabashed love. Susan Hamilton had told him she loved him, but never, even in their most intimate moments, had he been convinced that she was really sincere. He had always had the feeling that, to Susan, he was a matter of convenience. She wanted to marry a young officer to mold into her image of a husband, and Mark Shields fit the bill. But to be honest with himself, he had never been completely convinced that he really loved Susan.

He was not ready to admit that he loved Sasha either, though he already felt more for her, and felt it more deeply, than anything he had felt for Susan. And he knew without a doubt that if he did commit himself to her, her acceptance would be total and unequivocal. He suddenly—and unexpectedly —found himself kissing her.

Though Sasha knew the term, she had never been kissed. Kissing was not common among the Indians, so it was not something she ever thought about, even in her fantasies. But when she felt Shields's lips over hers, she was amazed at the sensations it evoked. Her head started spinning, and then she felt his tongue, brushing across her lips. Her body was warmed with a heat she had never before experienced, and her head grew so light that she abandoned all thought save this solitary pleasure. It was a condition she would have gladly extended indefinitely, but finally Shields broke off the kiss, leaving her standing as limp as a rag doll.

"I'm . . . I'm sorry," Shields mumbled in apology. "I don't know what came over me."

Sasha touched her lips with her fingertips, still feeling the tingling sensations there. She looked at Shields with eyes clouded with passion.

"You kissed me. Is that what white people do to their women?" she asked quietly.

"Yes," Shields said.

Sasha smiled broadly. "I like it," she said. "And it means I am your woman, does it not?"

Shields looked at her for a long moment, and then he smiled. "Yes," he said. "It means you are my woman."

Sasha pushed her lips out in a pout. "You may do it again," she said.

Shields chuckled and lay his forefinger across her lips. "Not now, little one," he said gently. "It's nearly time for assembly. We'll be pulling out soon, and I have some work to do."

"When you leave," Sasha said solemnly, "my heart will ride with you."

As always, the entire fort eagerly turned out for the departure of the expeditionary force early that afternoon. The officers and men who were not going had been given temporary leave from their duties to form a parade front under the flagpole in the quadrangle. The civilians, wives, visitors to the post, and Farley Branson stood in the sally port watching the proceedings. Sasha was standing with her father just outside the hospital.

Shields was on horseback. He was second in command, behind Captain Ross, who personally was leading the expedition. For the moment there was absolute silence. The only sound that could be heard was the snapping and flapping of the garrison flag flying high overhead.

"Executive officer, post!" Captain Ross called, and Shields rode to the front of the formation and took his position. Behind him, sitting tall and proud in their saddles, were one hundred and fifty cavalrymen.

"Executive officer, under your command pass the column in review," Ross ordered. That meant that Shields would move the troops by in parade formation while Captain Ross, in position under the flagpole, would receive a salute. It was actually an honor reserved for field-grade rank only, but as post commander Ross took the honor for himself.

"Form column of twos!" Shields shouted, his voice echoing across the fort.

The men executed the command.

"Guidon, post!" he yelled, and a soldier carrying a red-and-white swallowtail pennant galloped to the head of the column in front of the men and stopped just behind Shields.

"Column left, ho!" Shields commanded, and the formation paraded smartly around the square and passed in review before Ross, the band, the remaining troops of the post, and the assembled civilians.

As the column rode past Ross, Shields drew his saber and gave the command, "Eyes right!" He held the hilt of the sword at his chin with the blade pointing up and out at a forty-five-degree angle and turned his head to the right to pay his respects to the commander. Ross returned his salute, and the band broke into a stirring march. Shields looked forward and returned his saber to the scabbard just as they moved through the gates, and then he halted to wait for Ross to join the column and assume command.

When the column had moved completely out of sight and the troops assembled on the parade ground were dismissed, Sasha walked out to the signal cannon. She stood there quietly for a long moment. It was a good place to be while thinking of Shields, since they had shared so many moments there. She was sad that he was gone but happy because he had told her that she was his woman. Lost in her thoughts and memories, she did not hear the soft footfalls approaching.

"Well, that was quite a grand parade, wasn't it?" Branson said, coming up to her and startling her.

"Yes," she said as she recovered her composure.

Branson stood with his hands on his hips, looking out through the gate in the direction the troops had gone.

"Yes, sir," he went on. "We're finally going to get some action around here now. There won't be any more Indian trouble. I believe you can count on that."

"It will be good not to have trouble between the Indians and the whites," Sasha agreed.

Branson looked thoughtfully at Sasha for a moment and stroked his chin. "Sasha, I can talk to you," he said in a warm, confidential tone. "I know how much you care for Chatoma. I know he's been like a father to you."

"He is my father," Sasha corrected him firmly.

"Yes, well, the thing is, he doesn't understand the seriousness of the situation here," he went on smoothly, ignoring her tone of voice. "I made him an offer for his land grants, and he refused me. I want you to talk to him, to tell him that my offer is still good."

"If he would not sell before, why do you think he would sell now?" Sasha asked.

Branson smiled, a humorless, unpleasant leer. "Well, the situation is quite different now, isn't it? You see, he had better sell to me now, or the army will just take everything away from him anyway. This time there will be no restrictions. Like I said, Captain Ross has embarked upon an expedition to rid us of the Indian problem once and for all. That means all Indians, and all Indian land. You tell your father."

He did not pause for her reply but turned on his heels and walked off toward the sutler's store.

Sasha watched him walk away, disheartened and disturbed by both his words and his tone. Shields had promised her that he would do nothing against her people, but she realized that Shields was not the one in charge. If Captain Ross wished to do all that Branson said, he could do it, and Shields would be able to do nothing to prevent it.

Branson wanted her to take his words to her father, but Chatoma was just now beginning to recover, and she had no wish to upset him again. She decided she would say nothing about it.

Chapter Ten

Late that afternoon, Captain Ross decided to divide his forces into two groups, sending one third of the men with Shields, while he took the remaining two thirds with him.

"I will go west, to strike at the heart of the enemy," Ross said as he gave his orders to Shields. "You go north to see that they don't escape."

"Captain, my patrols have thoroughly scouted west all the way to the Santa Maria River," Shields said in protest. "There are no hostiles in that direction."

"Have you been able to locate the hostiles, Lieutenant?" Ross asked him, a condescending smile playing at the corners of his lips.

"No, sir." Shields flushed. He knew where this line of questioning was leading.

"Then you don't know where they are, do you?" Ross said sternly.

"No, sir," Shields said contritely. "I suppose not."

"Then I suggest you leave the tactics to me. I'm a little more experienced than you."

"Yes, sir," Shields said. He saluted Ross. "By your leave, sir, I shall withdraw now."

"Very good. We will rendezvous at Fort Verde in three days." Ross turned and rode away.

"Yes, sir," Shields muttered at his back, a disquieting feeling growing in him.

Shields and O'Braugh had been riding at the head of the

troop in a tense silence for the better part of an hour when Shields at last shared his concern over Ross's orders.

"Don't you think it a little strange that he sent us off like this with instructions that we wouldn't rejoin him until we returned to the post?" Shields asked, a puzzled frown creasing his broad forehead.

"I must admit, sir, 'tis not normal tactical procedure," O'Braugh said carefully.

"I have a bad feeling about this, Sergeant Major. I think Captain Ross was trying to get rid of us."

"For what purpose?" O'Braugh asked.

"I don't know, O'Braugh. I just don't know."

Suddenly one of the advance scouts Shields had sent out came galloping back toward them, urging his horse down the hill at breakneck speed. Shields held his hand up to halt the column to wait for the rider. The soldier pulled his horse up short, just in front of Shields.

"Lieutenant, I spotted 'em, sir," the wide-eyed rider said frantically. "They's near a hunnert of 'em, just ahead. And they's the one's we're lookin' for too, 'cause I seen ole' Manitoro hisself."

"One hundred!" Shields exclaimed, astounded. "Jackson, are you sure of your numbers?"

"Yes, sir, I'm sure. An' that's just the warriors. They's women and kids and old men with 'em, too. They's nigh on three hunnert in the village," Jackson went on excitedly.

"You know what that means, Sergeant Major?" Shields spun around to face O'Braugh. "We've found the main body. There Ross is, on some wild-goose chase, when actually all the Indians are up here!"

"Shall we send a messenger, sir?" O'Braugh asked.

"Yes." Shields nodded, and he reached into his tunic and pulled a small pad and pencil from its pocket. He rapidly scribbled a note on a pad; then, scanning the faces of the men in his column, he called for a volunteer. A small, wiry man rode up to him. He was known as the best rider of the troop, and Shields was glad he had volunteered, for he was just the man he wanted to carry the message.

"Get this to Captain Ross," Shields said. "Tell him to come quickly. We've located Manitoro and his main body."

"Yes, sir," the messenger said, taking the note from Shields. He folded it, stuck it in his tunic pocket, and then turned his horse and began galloping away, riding so swiftly that within moments he was just a dot on the horizon.

"Kenny's a good lad, Lieutenant," O'Braugh said, watching the man ride away. "He'll get through."

Shields nodded to O'Braugh, and then turning to the scout, he asked, "Jackson, how far away are the Indians?"

"They've got a camp set up about three miles ahead, sir!"

"Do you think they've spotted us?"

"No, sir, I don't think so," Jackson answered. "They weren't showin' no signs of movin'."

Shields looked around at his men and began assessing the situation. There were only fifty of them . . . fifty against Manitoro's band of one hundred warriors. Since the warriors would be defending their camp and their families, they would be particularly ferocious if the cavalry attacked them now. The best thing, he decided, was to move his men into a good defensive position, just in case they were discovered, and wait for Ross. If Manitoro tried to move his camp, Shields and his men would be able to follow them.

"All right," Shields said, scanning the terrain and pointing to a nearby hill. "Let's get into position there. We'll wait for Ross."

"Yes, sir," O'Braugh said, and he began passing the order on to the men. Within half an hour, Shields's column had established a defensive position on the hill.

In the deepening twilight the men made a cold camp, which meant that with no fires they had no coffee or cooked food. O'Braugh strolled over to Shields, carved off a piece of jerky, and handed it to him. He eased his big frame to the ground and settled down beside him.

"Do you ever wish things could be different?" Shields asked, and he looked over at O'Braugh with a thoughtful look on his face.

"In what way, sir?"

"Well, like now, for instance," Shields said. "Tomorrow we'll be doing battle against the Indians—savages, heathen, hostiles, people call them. But having met Chatoma and knowing Sasha, even though she isn't really an Indian, I've learned a few things."

O'Braugh chuckled quietly. "That they're people, you mean? Like you and me?"

"Yes. And I think they're fighting for what they believe in . . . even Manitoro and his followers. I don't know, maybe I shouldn't talk about it . . . shouldn't think about it. Tomorrow I'll be killing them, and if I stop to think about it, I don't know if I'll be able to do it."

"Killin's never easy, no matter who it is," O'Braugh said. "You take the Civil War. In that war, ever'one was killin' his own kind, with no ambitions from the war other than stayin' alive."

"Yet you stayed in the army after the war was over," Shields observed.

"Aye, lad. The army is my home. It's family an' church an' country, all rolled into one. The army takes care of its own."

"Like Ross?" Shields asked.

"I know you don't like Ross, and maybe you've a good reason not to," O'Braugh said. "But the army's no different from anyplace else. Some of us are good, some are bad. Some are brave, and some are cowards. But we're all goin' to wind up in Fiddlers' Green sooner or later."

"Fiddlers' Green?"

O'Braugh looked surprised. "Sure, lad, and you'd be knowin' about Fiddlers' Green? That fancy school on the Hudson wouldn't have neglected that part of your learnin'."

"I'm afraid they have," Shields replied.

"Fiddlers' Green is a quiet, cool glen, set under trees alongside a bubbling brook," O'Braugh said quietly. "It's halfway between heaven and hell, and ever' man that's ever heard the bugle play 'Boots and Saddles' goes there when he dies. Custer's there, and Fetterman, and your father himself. They'll wait there, you see, bein' served drinks in silver goblets, tellin' tall tales to one another until final assembly is blown, and they're all together so as to march into heaven in parade formation." O'Braugh chuckled. "That way, you see, we'll be able to sneak a few of our mates in that wouldn't otherwise be let into heaven, bein' as St. Peter wouldn't be wantin' a smart cavalry formation to break ranks now, would he?"

"Fiddlers' Green," Shields said, smiling at him. "Sounds like a nice place."

"It's comfortin' to think about," O'Braugh agreed.

* * *

As the shadows of twilight deepened into night and lanterns were lit in Sedona, a depressed Emily Rourke stood on the darkened porch in front of her office, listening to the sounds of celebration. Down the entire length of the street, jubilant noises burst from the saloons. The songs from half a dozen pianos competed with one another in the din of clinking glasses and boisterous laughter. Someone got a bit too rowdy somewhere, and Emily heard the crash of glass, possibly a mirror or one of the expensive chandeliers that had been shipped from the East. The crash was followed by loud cursing and more deep-throated laughter.

Sedona was celebrating because the army was on the move, and as snippets of conversation reached her ears, she heard that the townsmen shared the same ugly sentiments.

"Send the dirty redskins down to San Carlos where they belong."

"We don't need any Indians around here."

"The only good Indian is a dead Indian."

Shaking her head disgustedly, Emily started back into her office to return to the paperwork on her desk. Out of the corner of her eye, in the light cast on the boardwalk by saloon lanterns, she spied two old Suni Indians struggling with a group of townsmen. She knew the Indians. They were frequent visitors, coming to Sedona to earn a little money by selling firewood. Horrified, Emily watched as the drunken townsmen—a so-called Citizens' Committee—tarred and feathered the old men and then ran them out of town, accompanied by the shouts and laughter of nearly three dozen drunken cowboys.

Emily could take no more of it. Shaking with rage, she hastily closed the office and harnessed the team to her wagon. She left town and drove as fast as she could to Fort Verde. During the drive Emily gradually began to calm down, the cool evening air and the steady, soothing sound of the horses hooves bringing her a measure of peace. She arrived at the post just as the bugler was blowing retreat and the colors were being struck.

Dora McCorkle was the first to see Emily and hurried out to greet her. Other wives whose husbands were in the field joined the two women, and when one of them suggested that they all eat together, it turned into a party of sorts. The group approached Amy Hartfield, whose house was the only one large enough to accommodate all of them, and she, delighted by the excuse to gather, happily invited all of them in.

Each of the ladies prepared a special dish for the supper, and the happy chatter of half a dozen women filled the Hartfields' house. After the meal had been eaten and the ladies were all sitting around Amy Hartfield's well-lighted parlor, one of the women asked Emily if she missed the army.

"Yes," Emily said, surprised to hear herself say the word. "I think I do."

"Ha," Julie Bates said. "You can't tell me you miss the long time between paydays." The others laughed with her.

"As a matter of fact, I do," Emily replied. She smiled. "Perhaps not in the same way . . . I don't like being without money any more than anyone else does. But if you think about it, everyone is in the same boat when that happens. And if it is a sort of 'misery loves company' feeling, then I must say that you were all good company."

"I know one thing," Amy said, smiling at Emily warmly. "We sure miss you."

Everyone agreed. Then Dora looked directly at Emily. "All right," she said, her eyes sparkling mischievously. "Now that that is all settled, it's time to ask the question."

"The question? What question?" Emily asked, wide-eyed.

"The big question," Dora said. "Why don't you marry Kevin O'Braugh?"

To her surprise, Emily actually felt herself blushing. She was speechless.

"Well?" Dora insisted.

"Maybe it's because he hasn't asked me," Emily finally said. She looked down at her hands to conceal her embarrassment and discovered that they were twisting a portion of her skirt into wrinkles.

"Well, if that's all it takes, you leave that to me," Dora said with a howling laugh. "I'll take care of that little thing."

"Ladies, ladies, let's not push her into anything she doesn't want," Amy said quickly.

"It's all right, Mrs. Hartfield," Emily said as she looked up once more at the smiling faces of her friends. "I know my first husband would approve most heartily. And it isn't something I don't want." She was unable to believe she was really speaking the words.

"Well," one of the other wives said. "It's time I got back home. With our men in the field, I have to keep a closer watch over the children."

"Ladies," Dora said quietly. "Don't forget. Tonight before you go to sleep . . . a little prayer for our men." She looked over at Emily and added, "For all of our men."

Gathering their pots and pans and thanking Amy Hartfield warmly, the ladies left for their own homes, and Emily was left alone with the hostess.

"I, uh, apologize for barging in on you like this," she said, embarrassed that she had fled Sedona without considering the consequences of her abrupt departure. "But I had to get away from town, and now I find I have no place to stay the night."

"Well, you'll stay right here," Amy said warmly. "You can share the room with Sasha."

"Oh, I hate to put her out," Emily protested.

"Don't be silly, dear," Amy said, shaking her head. "Sasha thinks the world of you. I know she would be very pleased to share the room with you. She's visiting her father right now, but she'll be back in here soon, and she can help get you settled." She smiled to assure her.

"Thank you," Emily said, relieved. "I can't tell you how much I appreciate that."

Captain Ross's scouts had discovered an Indian village just before nightfall, and he had given the order to go into bivouac to wait for darkness and the opportunity to attack.

"The Indians may not believe in attack at night," he told Sergeant McCorkle, "but I see it as a tactical necessity. We may be outnumbered, but if we execute the plan carefully, the numbers won't matter."

"Captain Ross," Sergeant McCorkle said. "What are you going to do about the message we received from Lieutenant Shields this afternoon?"

"What am I going to do about it? Nothing, that's what," Ross said airily.

"But he asked us to come," McCorkle protested. "Sir, he's found Manitoro. Isn't that who we're looking for?"

Captain Ross fixed an angry stare at McCorkle.

"We don't know that he found Manitoro," he said. Ross pointed in the direction of the village, which was about three miles from their bivouac. "For all we know, he may be in this village."

"Sir, that ain't really very likely, is it?" McCorkle asked. "I mean, we are a way off the track."

"Exactly my point, Sergeant," Ross explained patiently. "Why haven't we been able to find Manitoro and his people before now? Because they aren't where we expected them to be. Well, I believe we have found them here."

"But this ain't no war camp," McCorkle insisted.

"Oh? And how did you reach that conclusion, Sergeant?"

"I rode up there and looked around. Cap'n, they ain't got enough horses to seat more'n a dozen men at any one time. And I seen a garden."

"If Manitoro is clever enough to set up his camp out of the normal area, don't you think he is also clever enough to disguise that camp?" Ross asked indignantly.

"And Lieutenant Shields?"

"Sergeant, do I have to remind you that I am in command, not Lieutenant Shields? I will accept his message for exactly what it is . . . a piece of information submitted from a subordinate to his commander. But as the commander I will act on my own. And my orders are, at three o'clock in the morning we will attack the Indian village that we located today," he said firmly and turned away.

"Yes, sir," McCorkle said, and he sighed deeply and shook his head. He had carried the argument as far as he could. From this point on the only thing he could do was be the proper soldier and noncommissioned officer, and that meant obeying the orders of his superior.

At three o'clock the next morning, Ross sat in his saddle and looked down toward the sleeping Indian village. There was absolutely no sign of life.

"They don't even have any guards out," McCorkle said, appalled.

"Good. Our element of surprise is complete," Ross replied.

"You want to wait till just after sunrise to attack?" McCorkle asked, hoping to buy some time. Captain Ross might come to his senses.

"No, Sergeant, I don't. Why should I want to do that? It

could compromise the element of surprise we have worked so hard to achieve."

"I was just thinkin' on the women and children," McCorkle said softly.

"And what, exactly, were you thinking about them?" Ross snapped.

"In the dark, sir, it might be hard to tell them apart from the warriors. There's bound to be some women and children get themselves killed."

"We are at war with them, Sergeant McCorkle. And I would like to remind you of a favorite statement of Custer's. 'Nits make lice.' What that means, Sergeant, is if we let the little ones grow up, we'll just have to fight them sometime in the future. Why not get rid of all of them now?"

McCorkle turned away and swallowed hard to force the bitter taste down.

In the shadows of the wickiups before them, the soldiers noticed a lone figure stirring. The figure walked over to a well. After pulling up a bucket of water from it, the figure slipped out of a blanket and began bathing in the privacy of the predawn darkness. The soldiers saw that it was a young, shapely woman.

The men watched in silence as the young woman went about her ablutions, completely unaware that her every move was being devoured by over one hundred pairs of eyes. Then, as if feeling something on her, she looked up and stared directly at the spot where the soldiers were hidden.

"Shoot her now," Ross ordered gruffly. "If she sees us and gives the alarm, the surprise will be over."

"Yes, sir," a nearby sharpshooter said. "Watch me. I bet I can get her right between the eyes." He drew his rifle from his saddle scabbard, crossed one leg over his saddle, then leaned forward to rest his elbow on his leg while he took slow, deliberate aim. There was a long, pregnant silence as the young woman at the well continued her bathing, unaware that she was in the last seconds of her life.

The rifle boomed and rocked back against the marksman's shoulder. Even from this distance the men could see the woman's head explode as the bullet crashed into it.

"Trumpeter! Sound the charge!" Ross ordered.

As the notes rang out, one hundred cavalrymen swept forward, firing rifles and pistols and screaming bloodcurdling, defiant shouts. The Indians, startled from a peaceful sleep by the sound of the first shot, came running from their wickiups, only to be cut down by rifle or pistol fire. When they were too close to the Indians to fire, the soldiers slashed at them, either with sabers or with their rifles, crushing necks and severing heads. Women were murdered without mercy, and children and babies run down and trampled. Old men and unarmed warriors were killed, and the wickiups were burned.

"All right, men, that's enough!" Ross shouted. "Trumpeter, sound recall."

The trumpeter played as ordered, and the cavalrymen who had been riding to and fro in the village dealing out death and destruction suddenly stopped their systematic slaughter and withdrew from the field. Behind them, they could hear cries of anguish and grief coming from those Indians who had survived the massacre. When they reached the top of the hill, Ross turned to look back at his handiwork. More than forty wickiups had been burned, and many were still in flames. They looked like burning beehives in the predawn darkness.

"My God, what a victory I've won here tonight!" Ross cried.

When McCorkle looked into Ross's eyes, they were brightly lit and dancing with the reflection of the flames of the village. But that was not what McCorkle saw at all—he was looking directly into the eyes of a madman.

"Lieutenant! Lieutenant! Here they come!"

The sentry's cries woke Shields from a fitful, uneasy sleep. He sat up quickly, in time to see at least a hundred mounted Indians riding toward him and his men. The Indians were screaming loudly, and some were already beginning to fire their rifles.

"Sergeant Major!" Shields shouted. "Move the men to skirmish lines!"

"Men!" O'Braugh shouted, repeating Shields's order. "To your positions!"

"Fire on my command!" Shields yelled, and he pulled his pistol and aimed it at the approaching horde.

Suddenly he saw something black, like a flight of birds, coming from behind the attacking Indians. At the last moment he realized with a sense of horror that it was a cloud of arrows. Whereas bullets traveled in a straight trajectory and could be turned aside by the rocks and the parapets the men had constructed during the night, the arrows flew in a long arc, rising above the defenses and dropping right onto the men. Half a dozen soldiers shouted in pain as the arrows found their marks.

"Stand steady, men!" Shields cautioned. "Hold your fire!"

The mounted Indians continued their attack, firing their rifles at the soldiers, although unlike the arrows none of the bullets found a target. Another cloud of arrows was loosed, but this time the men were ready for them, and they traced their arc all the way in, stepping aside at the last moment to avoid being hit. One of the arrows stuck into the ground right between Shields's feet.

The attacking Indians had ridden close enough to be within pistol range, and Shields knew that meant his men armed with carbines should not miss.

"Fire!" he yelled, feeling his pistol buck in his hand. There was a ripple of fire from the soldiers around him, and then the sound of levers worked as new rounds were jacked into the chambers.

The soldiers were armed with repeating rifles so that they were able to fire a second volley immediately following the first. Shields knew that Custer's men had been equipped with single-shot, breech-loading carbines, and in many cases one shot was all any of them got. Though Shields had only fifty men with him, his fifty were as effective as all two hundred of Custer's had been . . . and he was facing not thousands of Indians but only one hundred.

More than a dozen Indians tumbled from their horses on the first volley; another dozen were hit by the second volley. In less than ten seconds the Indian attack force had been reduced by one fourth, although Manitoro, leading the charge, had not been hit. Nevertheless, Manitoro suddenly realized that he was at a disadvantage, so he whirled about and led his warriors off the field of battle, leaving his dead and dying behind him.

Manitoro's scouts had discovered Shields's presence during the night. In preparation for the battle Manitoro had ordered all the women and children to sneak away from the encampment long before dawn had broken. Though they had taken the bare necessities, the wickiups were left in place so the soldiers would not realize what was happening. Manitoro had hoped that a charge by a force twice as large as the army's would drive the soldiers away. He was shocked to see that the army not only withstood his charge but also managed to kill many of his warriors.

With Manitoro at the head, the warriors swept back through his own camp. Manitoro stopped, took a firebrand from one of the several small fires, and tossed it onto a wickiup. Other Indians followed his lead, and within a matter of seconds the entire camp was ablaze. That was all they could do, because the soldiers had mounted and were now coming after them. Manitoro gave the order for his men to scatter. He knew from past experience that the soldiers, who preferred to stay in one body, would not split up to follow them.

Manitoro rode off alone, driving his horse until he thought the animal's heart would burst. When he looked over his shoulder, he saw that he was making good his escape. The soldier-chief had halted his men at the camp.

"Sergeant Major," Shields ordered, "see if you can find anything undamaged. We'll take whatever is left back to Fort Verde, and if any civilians recognize their belongings, we'll return them."

"Yes, sir," O'Braugh said. O'Braugh gave the orders, and the soldiers dismounted and began picking among the debris of the camp and locating various household items, which they pulled away from the fires and stacked up for removal.

"Lieutenant, would you be lookin' at this now," O'Braugh called a few minutes later. He was walking toward Shields, who stood near the remains of a campfire in the heart of the camp, and holding a piece of paper out to him.

"What is it?"

"The damnedest thing, Lieutenant," O'Braugh said, frowning and shaking his head. " 'Tis a map."

"A map?" Shields asked, puzzled.

"Aye, sir, a map. And on it is marked ever' place the heathen have attacked. See? There is the Webb ranch," he said, pointing to a spot on the paper.

"Look at this," Shields said, surprised. "That's the way

station between Prescott and Fort Verde. It's marked, but it hasn't been attacked."

"No, sir, an' neither has the Dumey ranch, but it's marked, too. But, see, it's a different kind of mark. These are places that the Indians plan to attack."

"It looks like they are concentrating everything on a line between Prescott and Sedona," Shields said. Frowning, he scratched his head. "Sergeant Major, you have more experience than I. Is it normal for an Indian to have a battle map like this?"

"I've been fightin' Indians a long time, sir," O'Braugh said, examining the map, "and I've never yet seen one who used a map. There's somethin' more'n a little peculiar about all this." He looked up at Shields.

"I don't know what to make of it, but I think I'd better take this back to the fort and let Captain Ross take a look at it."

O'Braugh handed the map back to Shields and then took a drink from his canteen. He offered his canteen to the lieutenant, who, with a word of thanks, also took a drink.

High in the rocks, Manitoro angrily looked down on the burning village that had been his safe camp. He watched as the soldiers salvaged his booty, and he saw the sergeant and the lieutenant ponder the map. Then he saw something that caused him to gasp aloud, and he felt a cold fear descend over him: He saw the young lieutenant take a drink of water. From his angle, however, it looked as if the lieutenant had reached down to dip the water right out of one of the fires that was still burning. That was exactly like the scene in his vision!

Shaken by what he had seen, Manitoro sat down behind the rock and tried to think what to do next. He realized, finally, that there was only one thing he could do. He had to kill the lieutenant, and he had to kill him with his own hands.

Chapter Eleven

The trip back to Fort Verde was grim and arduous for Shields and his men. Two of the six wounded men died on the way back to the post; another was so badly injured that the column had to stop and the men had to construct a travois for him. The other three were less seriously hurt, and although their wounds were painful, the men were able to sit their horses for the ride back. When they rode up to the fort, Shields turned and saw that his weary, dust-covered men showed the effects of the battle and the long ride back.

As Shields rode through the gate, the first thing he noticed was that the command pennant was flying on the pole in front of the headquarters building, announcing that Captain Ross had returned. The post was full of soldiers, many more than the few who had been left in the garrison when the troops departed. The next thing that caught his attention was the puzzling presence of civilians—nearly as many civilians as there were soldiers—and the civilians were in a festive mood.

"Sergeant Major, what do you make of this?" Shields asked, frowning at O'Braugh as they rode across the quadrangle.

"Tell you the truth, sir, I wouldn't be knowin' what to make of it," O'Braugh answered. He saw Emily's coach sitting near the wagon park. "But I'll be for findin' out shortly. There's Mrs. Rourke's coach."

"Three cheers for the army!" one of the civilians shouted as Shields brought his command up to the flagpole. "Hip, hip, hooray! Hip, hip, hooray! Hip, hip, hooray!" The civilian who had started the cheer was joined by others, and they actually applauded as Shields turned the command over to O'Braugh to dismiss the men.

As Shields dismounted, he heard O'Braugh issue the order for some of the men to take the wounded to the hospital. After entering the headquarters buildings, the lieutenant went into the orderly room.

The clerk stood and smiled at him. "Welcome back, sir," he said.

"What's going on?" Shields asked. "Why so many civilians?"

"Why, they're celebratin', sir," the clerk said with a wide grin.

"Celebrating? Celebrating what?" Shields asked, a puzzled frown creasing his forehead.

"Celebrating Captain Ross's victory over the Indians. There was a hell of a fight, sir, and we whipped 'em. We whipped 'em good."

"A fight? My God, whom did he fight?"

"I fought Manitoro," Ross said, appearing in the doorway of his office at that moment. He was smiling broadly and openly carrying a drink. He held the glass up. "Come on in, Lieutenant. Come on in and help us celebrate!"

Shields, incredulous at what he was hearing and seeing, followed Ross into his office. There he saw Branson and a couple of the men he had seen in the delegation from Sedona the other day. Like the captain, they were smiling broadly and drinking. Only Branson was not holding a glass, but it suddenly dawned on Shields that he had never seen Branson drink.

"I'm glad you're back, Lieutenant," Ross said, waving his drink as he spoke. "I was beginning to think I would have to send a search party out to look for you. Of course, you wouldn't have been the first shavetail to get lost out here." He laughed and winked at the civilians, who joined in the laughter.

"Captain Ross, what's going on here?" Shields asked.

"What's going on? Why, a celebration, that's what. The townspeople have brought in fried chicken, pies, cakes, and unattached young women." He smiled and winked again. "The men will have a picnic this afternoon, and tonight there will be a dance at the sutler's. Oh, I suspect this is a day we won't soon forget."

"Tell the lieutenant what the celebration is all about, Captain. Don't be so modest," one of the civilians said.

Ross smiled broadly and walked over to the map behind his desk. "Right here," he said, gesturing at the map with his glass, "at the foot of Granite Peak. That's where we found him. I knew he would have to be there; we had looked everywhere else. That was the only place he could be."

"You found whom, sir?" Shields asked, straining to be patient.

"Why, Manitoro and his heathens. I found his main camp, Shields. I found his warriors, shaman, wives, supplies, everything. And I hit the bastard. I hit him hard!" Ross punched the air wildly with his free hand, spilling some of the whiskey from the glass he held in the other.

"Captain, are you saying Manitoro's main camp is all the way over near Granite Peak?" Shields gave him a dubious glance.

"Well, not anymore, it ain't," one of the civilians chimed in. "Captain Ross took care of it."

"I told you I hit him hard. Knowing that Indians don't like to fight at night, that's exactly when we attacked, in the middle of the night," Ross said as he set his glass on the desk. "There are a few of the heathen bastards wandering around looking for their souls now, you can believe." Smiling, he rubbed his hands together proudly. "I've already wired the news of my success to Washington. Unlike Custer, Shields, I didn't lose a man, not one. On the other hand, I would estimate enemy casualties at sixty-five to seventy percent. Not only that, the ones who got away are so scattered that never again will they form an effective fighting force." Ross saw the look of surprise on Shields's face, and he chuckled. "What's the matter, boy? Did you think I was just a garrison soldier?"

"Captain Ross, didn't you receive the message I sent you? I told you I had Manitoro located and would wait for your support before attacking," Shields said icily.

"Oh, yes, I received it," Ross said airily. "But by the time I got your message, I had already found Manitoro's actual camp, so I realized you had made a mistake."

"A mistake?" Shields was incredulous.

"Yes. Oh, I'm sure you found a camp of some sort . . . probably a hunting camp, and you assumed it was Manitoro. I don't fault you for it, Lieutenant; after all, you're new to Indian fighting and under stress could quite easily make such a mistake. War camps and hunting camps do look quite a bit alike. Don't worry, I promise I won't put it on your efficiency report," Ross assured him.

"I don't know who the Indians were that you slaughtered, Captain Ross, but they didn't belong to Manitoro. I fought Manitoro, and unlike you, I didn't come away without casualties. I had two killed and four wounded, one seriously."

"Look here, are you saying you saw Manitoro?" one of the civilians asked.

"That's exactly what I'm saying," Shields said firmly.

"Lieutenant, did you kill or capture Manitoro?" Ross asked.

"No, sir, he got away."

Ross smiled. "Then you don't really know, do you? He did get away, Lieutenant, but not from your battle, from mine. However, we will get him, in time. And in the meantime, we're going to make the entire valley, from Prescott to Sedona, Indian-free."

"What do you mean by that?" Shields looked at him sharply.

"I intend to remove all the Indians from here and place them on the reservation at San Carlos."

"All?" Shields's eyes narrowed.

"Every one."

"Including Chatoma's people?"

"Especially Chatoma's people."

Shields was stunned; he was so enraged that he felt he would explode. He slowly drew a deep breath to calm his flaring temper and sort his racing thoughts. Suddenly remembering the map he had found in Manitoro's tepee, Shields reached in his tunic to pull it out. "Captain, I would like to make an official report on the results of my patrol," he said.

"Go ahead."

"In private, if you don't mind, sir."

Ross sighed and then looked at the civilians who were guests in his office. "Gentlemen, I'm sorry," he said. "The lieutenant wants to make his report in private, and that is his right. Would you please excuse us?"

"Certainly," Branson said. "I'll see how preparations are going for the dance tonight." Branson looked pointedly at the map Shields was holding in his hand and glanced up at Shields, but he said nothing as he left the room.

"All right, what is it?" Ross asked once the other men had gone.

"Captain Ross, I want you to look at this map," Shields said, spreading the paper before Ross on his desk. "Notice that all the places that have been attacked by Manitoro are marked here."

"So?" Ross shrugged.

"Don't you find that a little unusual?"

Ross sighed and looked up at Shields. "Look at the map on the wall behind me, Lieutenant. I think you'll find the same thing."

"Yes, sir, but you are a military commander, and that is normal operating procedure. This was Manitoro's map. Have you ever heard of an Indian using a battle map?"

"No, and that should prove a point to you. That isn't an Indian's map, and it certainly doesn't belong to Manitoro, because you didn't encounter him," Ross said angrily.

"Sir, this came from his tent," Shields protested.

"Lieutenant, if I hear one more word from you, I will consider it an act of contempt of command," Ross raged at Shields. "You say you fought Manitoro; I say I fought him. Since neither of us have Manitoro to prove our claim, we must fall back on the only thing that matters." Ross smiled without humor, his eyes narrowed viciously. "Rank. And since I outrank you, that means that I fought Manitoro, and you did not. Now get out of my office, see to your wounded, and get cleaned up. We have many civilians on the post, and you are a disgrace to your uniform." Ross finished his tirade by downing the rest of his liquor.

Shields was so struck by the hypocrisy of the captain's "disgrace to the uniform" remark that he wanted to punch Ross. Instead, he gritted his teeth and let the vein in his temple throb while he controlled his temper. "Yes, sir," he said. He saluted sharply, did an about-face, and then left the office.

As promised, Captain Ross held a big dance that night at the sutler's store. The officers and soldiers were resplendently turned out in their dress uniforms, while the women—more women than ever before, because their numbers were boosted by the women from town—wore butterfly-bright gowns with cascades of colorful ribbon and golden earbobs, which sparkled and flashed from beneath the curls that dangled saucily from their heads.

Conspicuously absent from the dance was Sasha Quiet Stream. The dance was a celebration of the killing of many Indians, and even though they were not from her own village, she could not participate. Emily Rourke was there, but she and O'Braugh were silent observers only. O'Braugh was there by command, and Emily was there because he was. She had already had her fill of Indian baiting.

The music spilled outside the sutler's store and rolled across the quadrangle. The guards on the walls listened and tapped their feet in time to the music and thought of the beautiful young women inside. They cursed their luck at being on guard duty that night, and more than one of them stood at his post, not looking outward as he should, but back inside the fort toward the golden splash of light from the party. Overhead the stars shimmered like ice crystals, while behind them the Mazatzal Mountains were great slabs of black and silver in the soft wash of moonlight.

A sudden blaze of gold zipped across the sky, and in his hiding place among the boulders a hundred feet from the wall, Manitoro smiled. The meteor was a sign, a good sign for him, for its gold color matched the amulet he wore around his neck. He closed his blue eyes and touched it to feel its power. Breathing deeply, he felt great strength flow into his body. With a slow, confident smile, he opened his eyes and scanned the wall of the fort.

Seeing that the guard was still looking toward the sound of the music, he slipped from the concealing shadows of the boulders and darted across the open space between the rocks and the bottom of the wall. Silently, he threw a rawhide line up to the top of the wall, caught it on one of the sharpened palisades, and started climbing. When he reached the walkway on top, he crept slowly around the wall, bending low to blend with the shadows.

The guard was still watching the dance and inattentive. It was easy for Manitoro to slip up behind him, cup the guard's mouth with his left hand, and then with his right plunge a knife in under the ribs. The soldier made a grunting sound, more of surprise than of pain. Manitoro held him while he struggled, and when the struggling stopped, the victor lay him down silently. He removed the soldier's jacket and hat, picked up his carbine, and stood up. In the dark, only the shadowy silhouettes of the other guards could be seen. Anyone who looked over would not be alarmed, for he would see the guard still on duty.

"Post number one, and all is well!" The call floated across the quadrangle.

"Post number two, and all is well!"

"Post number three, and all is well."

A numbing silence followed. Manitoro felt a rush of anxiety. What was he supposed to do?

"Johnny? Johnny, you all right over there?" the nearest guard whispered hoarsely.

"Yeah," Manitoro answered in a guttural cough.

"Man, you better give the call for post number four, or the sergeant of the guard's gonna think you're sleepin' on duty."

Manitoro took a deep breath. "Post number four, and all is well!" he called.

"Post number five, and all is well!"

Manitoro smiled as he heard the call travel around all ten posts. He had fooled them. Now all he had to do was wait for the lieutenant who could drink water from fire.

Shields made an appearance at the party, but when he saw that Ross was so drunk that he would not know if the lieutenant were there, he left. He started across the moonlit quadrangle toward the hospital, hoping to find Sasha there. He noticed a slender figure standing near the signal cannon, and he smiled and started toward it.

"I hoped you would remember this place and come to see me," Sasha said softly, smiling up at him.

"I didn't forget," Shields said gently.

"I could not go to the party. I hope you do not mind."

Shields looked back toward the brightly lit sutler's store and shook his head. "I couldn't go, either," he said. "Ross is a fool."

"Do the other soldiers also believe he is a fool?"

"Yes," Shields said.

"Then I do not understand. Why is he still the chief of soldiers? Why do you not send him away?"

Shields laughed lightly. Sasha was right in her wonderfully simple way. "It isn't done like that. Come on, we'd better take a walk before you get me involved in an act of sedition."

Sasha smiled. "Yes," she said. "I would like to take a walk."

Shields offered his arm, and when Sasha did not know what to do with it, he put her hand through it to show her.

"Is this what men and women do in the world of the whites?" she asked.

Shields recalled the walks he had taken with Susan Hamilton along the Hudson River back at West Point. "Yes," he said, "I suppose it is."

"It is nice," Sasha said, pleasure and delight clear in her voice.

As they walked along the wall of the fort, Shields pointed to the ring she wore around her neck.

"Did that wedding ring belong to your mother?" he asked. "Your real mother?"

"Yes. And this is a lock of her hair. I have always worn it, though I can barely remember her. What did you call it? A wedding ring?"

"Yes. After the wedding, the woman wears that on her finger to show that she is married."

"And the men?"

"Yes, there are wedding rings for men, too."

"I did not know this," Sasha said. "When I am married, may I wear it on my finger? Or, since it belonged to my mother, does that mean I cannot?"

"No, many women wear the rings of their mothers."

"That is good. I will wear it when I am married. And I will get one for you to wear, too," she added.

Shields choked back a startled laugh. "You shouldn't say such things."

"Why? Do you not want to marry me?" Sasha looked at him with simple wonder.

"Maybe I do," Shields said, smiling at her innocence. "But it is for the man to ask."

"Mark . . . look out!" Sasha suddenly screamed.

Startled by the warning, Shields spun around just in

time to see a soldier coming toward him with a knife in his raised hand. Then he caught a glimpse of his painted face, and he realized that it was not a soldier—it was Manitoro!

Shields managed to lean aside just in time to avoid Manitoro's first rush. Manitoro missed him, but he turned toward the lieutenant, and this time the Indian lowered his arm and turned the knife so that he was holding it palm up. He stood in a wide stance, the point of the knife waving back and forth like the head of a snake. "I'm going to kill you, you snake," he snarled.

Shields had never heard Manitoro speak, and he was amazed at how well he used English.

Manitoro lunged with his knife. In one swift motion, Shields jumped aside and sent a quick, whistling right toward the Indian's nose. Manitoro was caught off guard and stunned by the blow. His nose started bleeding, and as he smiled a hate-filled leer at Shields, blood ran across his lips and his teeth, making him a frightening apparition to behold.

"Corporal of the guard!" Shields called, still staring at the leering Indian. "Post number four!" He heard the call repeated and then the sound of footsteps as other guards began running to respond to the alarm.

Suddenly Manitoro made another low slash with his knife, and again Shields managed to jump out of the way. Then, to Shields's shock and surprise, he saw Sasha suddenly leap upon Manitoro's back. With her arms and legs wrapped around him, she bit him on the ear, and he let out a howl of pain. The moment of distraction was all Shields needed. He reached out and was able to grab Manitoro's knife hand.

As Sasha slid off Manitoro's back, Shields struggled savagely to twist the knife from his hand. The two men were equally strong and evenly matched, and the outcome of the struggle was in doubt until two soldiers came running through the shadows toward them. One of the soldiers clubbed Manitoro on the back of the head, and the Indian collapsed, unconscious.

"Are you all right, sir?" the guard asked, panting from the effort of his run.

"Yes, thank you," Shields gasped as he worked to catch his breath. He looked over at Sasha. "Sasha, are you all right?"

"Yes."

"Don't ever do anything like that again," he said to her, more sharply than he intended. When he saw that she was hurt by his tone of voice, he softened his words. "On the other hand, you saved my life, and I want to thank you."

"Why, this here's Manitoro," one of the guards cried. "When I seen he was wearin' a uniform, I thought he was a soldier gone crazy."

"That's Johnny's jacket he's wearin'," a sentry called from up on the wall. "I just found him lyin' up here, dead."

"Get the jacket off him," Shields ordered sharply, pointing to the unconscious Manitoro. "I'll not have him desecrating the uniform."

One of the soldiers took the jacket off Manitoro, and when he did, Sasha gasped and pointed.

"What is it?" Shields asked, startled by her reaction.

"Around his neck," she cried. "He is wearing a ring like mine!"

Shields called for a lantern and knelt beside Manitoro. Slowly he lifted the gold ring and held it in his hand. In the lantern light he could see that the filigree design matched that of Sasha's ring exactly. He slowly shook his head.

"What does that mean?" Sasha asked.

Shields did not answer her. Lightly he put his hand on Manitoro's face. He could feel the stubble of a beard, and when he brushed away some of the war paint, he saw that the skin beneath was definitely white. He stood up slowly.

"Sasha, let's go talk to your father," he said firmly. "I think we should ask him a few questions."

"What do you want done with Manitoro, Lieutenant?"

"Put him in the guardhouse," Shields ordered.

Shields and Sasha started across the quadrangle toward the hospital. Word that Manitoro was on the grounds had reached the dance. Dozens of people—soldiers in full dress uniform and women holding the hems of their skirts up out of the dirt—were pouring out of the sutler's store. Wanting to avoid contact with everyone at this trying moment, Shields used the darkness and the shadows to slip unnoticed into the hospital with Sasha.

Chatoma was quiet for a long moment after Sasha told him about the discovery of a ring identical to hers around

Manitoro's neck. His brown eyes were deep and sad, and he suddenly looked very old.

"Listen," he finally said, "and I will tell a story."

Sasha had heard the old man begin many conversations in this way, for he was an adept storyteller, and this was the way he began when he wanted to teach lessons or to speak of something that was very difficult. She had an uneasy feeling that what he was about to tell would be difficult, not only for him to say but for her to hear.

"Once," Chatoma began, "there was a great chief of our people. His name was Keytano, and he made war against the Mexicans, and against the Navajo, and against the whites, and all who spoke of him said that he was a great warrior, with powerful medicine. His medicine made him not only a great warrior but a wise man as well, and when he grew old, he saw that the way of the warrior was passed. He had two sons, and he told his sons that they should follow the path of peace. One son did this; one son did not."

"You are the son who followed the path of peace," Sasha said.

"Yes. The son who did not follow in the path of peace was Kelaithe."

"I have heard of him," Shields said. "You mean he is your brother?"

"Yes," Chatoma said, nodding his head slowly. "Because Keytano knew that Kelaithe would choose the way of war rather than the path of peace, my father made me the new chief of our people. Kelaithe was very angry, and he left, vowing to fight always against the whites who would come to our country. Many of our people left with him, and the Tonto Apache became a people of two houses.

"Many years ago, some wagons came through our country. Some of my people feared that the wagons meant many whites would be coming to take our water, to hunt our buffalo, to use our land. We had a council, and at the council we agreed to let the wagons go, and in a few days they would be out of our country. But in Kelaithe's camp there was also a council, and in his council they said they would attack the wagons. This they did, and almost everyone was killed."

"That is the wagon train I was on, isn't it?" Sasha asked.

"Yes. When one of my braves came to me and told me what had happened, I went to the place where the wagons were burning, and I found a little girl. I took her and raised her as my own daughter. Then I went to my brother, and I had angry words for him for what he did. That was when I saw the little boy."

"The little boy?" Shields asked.

Sasha gasped. "Jimmy?" she whispered. Her brother's name, long buried in her past, suddenly leapt to her lips. "Jimmy was not killed?" she asked.

"Kelaithe did not see you because you were covered by the wagon. The boy was wounded, but he was not killed, so Kelaithe took him. I tried to take the boy, too, so you would be together. I offered Kelaithe six horses, but he would not let the boy come with me. Then, much later, when the boy was older, I spoke with him and told him of his sister. I asked him if he would come to live with us, but it was too late. He had been raised a warrior, and he would not listen."

"Manitoro," Sasha said softly, unbelievingly. "Manitoro is my brother."

"Yes," Chatoma said simply. His eyes were deep pools of sorrow as he looked at her.

Sasha's eyes filled with tears. "But why, Father? Why have you never told me of this?"

"It would bring only tears if you knew," Chatoma explained gently. "He would not leave the way of the warrior to come to you, and I did not want you to leave me to go with him."

Sasha put her arms around the old man's neck. "Father," she sobbed. "Do you really think I could have ever left you?"

"I should have told you," Chatoma whispered in a broken voice. "I am sorry."

When Shields and Sasha left the hospital, Sasha told him she wanted to talk to Manitoro.

"Why?" Shields asked. "I think Chatoma is right. I think it will only cause you more pain."

"Please, Mark. He is my brother. I must talk to him."

Shields suddenly remembered the map he had found in Manitoro's war camp, and he decided he would take this opportunity to confront Manitoro with it. "All right, you can talk to him," he agreed. "But I'm going with you. I have a few questions I want to ask him myself."

As they walked across the post to the guardhouse, they could hear the music from the sutler's store. The noises of the celebration were stronger than before, the party having been given more impetus by the capture of Manitoro. Shields heard a loud burst of laughter and the crashing tinkle of a bottle being smashed. Some of the celebration had moved out into the quadrangles away from the organized dance, and civilians and soldiers were there mingling and drinking together. Shields knew that could be a dangerous combination, and he hoped there would be no trouble.

The guard snapped to attention when Shields approached the guardhouse. The lieutenant returned his salute and then pointed toward the door.

"Let us in," he said. "I have a few questions I need to ask Manitoro, and the lady is going to help."

"Yes, sir," the guard said. He slipped the bar from the door, and Shields and Sasha went inside. By the light of the lantern burning inside, they could see Manitoro quite easily. Shields paused and studied him closely.

Sitting on the straw-covered floor of the guardhouse, Manitoro was leaning against the wall on the far side of the room. He glared at Shields and Sasha, his cobalt-blue eyes flashing at them. Now that Shields knew he was white, he wondered how he had ever thought of him as Indian.

"Jimmy?" Sasha said hesitantly.

Manitoro stared silently at her, his face totally impassive.

"You are my brother, Jimmy Mason, aren't you?"

Still no answer.

"You are older than I am. You can remember Mama and Papa better than I can. Surely you can," Sasha implored.

"I am not your brother," Manitoro said flatly.

"But you must be." Sasha pointed to the ring around his neck and then pulled out her own ring. "Look," she said. Her eyes pleaded with him. "We wear the same ring. This was Mama's ring. That must have been Papa's. Jimmy, I know you know who I am."

"I know you," he finally said.

"Oh, Jimmy, at last!" Sasha said, and before Shields could stop her, she had dashed across the room to put her arms around him.

Roughly he pushed her back and then spat at her feet. "Stay away from me!" he growled.

"Mister, do you really have that much hate in you?"

Shields demanded, as he made every effort to contain his anger.

Manitoro smiled evilly. "What do you know about hate?" he asked, his words hissing across the room. "I hate all whites, and I hate the 'white man's Apache' as much as I hate the white man."

"But you are white," Shields protested.

"No! I am Apache! I am Apache here," he said passionately as he touched his forehead. "And I am Apache here!" He put his hand to his heart.

"I, too, am Apache," Sasha said. "But I am also Lily Mason, a white woman, just as you are Jimmy Mason, a white man."

"If the whites had come when we were first captured," Manitoro said, "I would have been a white man. But the whites did not care. Where were the soldiers when we were children? They weren't here. I wanted them to come then." He laughed, though it was a mirthless, mocking laugh. "I even used to pray to the white man's God for them to come. But they did not come. And so I became Apache. And when I became Apache, I became the best Apache. I had many fights with other children because my skin was white. At night I would be in too much pain to sleep, but I wouldn't let anyone know. Then, because I fought many times, I became a good fighter. I could beat any one of the others, then many of the others together. I could fight better, ride harder, run faster than anyone. I became a warrior, then a chief. And now, everyone is afraid when they hear the name Manitoro."

"And that's what you want? You want everyone to be afraid of your name?" Shields asked.

"Everyone is afraid," Manitoro said haughtily.

"Mister, if that's what you wanted, that's what you've got," Shields said. "And if you want to be Manitoro, be Manitoro. But I must tell you, there is something strange about all this. There is a white man involved in this somewhere, for some reason, and I don't know why. Maybe you can tell me. Why were you using a map? And what is significant about the places you have attacked?"

"I will tell you nothing," Manitoro said, sneering. "Even if you torture me, I will tell you nothing."

"You have a lot to learn about the people you abandoned," Shields said. "We don't torture our prisoners to get information. If you won't tell me, I'll find out from someone else."

Sasha looked at Manitoro for a long moment. Then she wiped the tears away. "The tears were for my brother, Jimmy Mason," she said. "For the man who murders innocent people, and innocent children," she added, recalling the McAlister children who had been killed at Milo Pass, "I have no tears."

She looked at Manitoro for one long, sorrow-filled moment and then turned and left the guardhouse. Shields shook his head and followed her. He signaled to the guard to lock the door behind them.

As they were leaving, Captain Ross approached them from the shadows. Shields saw that he was carrying a bottle of whiskey in his hand and was so drunk he could barely stand.

"What were you doing in there?" he slurred at Shields.

"I was interrogating the prisoner about the map I found in his tent," Shields said. "You remember, Captain. I told you about it."

"And I told you that wasn't Manitoro's tent." Ross's voice rose to an angry shout. "I did battle with Manitoro, and I was more than twenty miles away from you. I don't know what map you have, but Manitoro has nothing to do with it."

"Captain, don't you think we ought to at least question him about it?" Shields asked evenly.

"And what was she doing in there?" Ross asked, pointing at Sasha with the hand that held the bottle and ignoring Shields's question.

"Manitoro is her brother," Shields said.

"Her brother?" Ross staggered.

"Yes, sir. I thought she might be able to help me get some information from him."

"That's what you tell me. Maybe it's something else," Ross said, waving his hand.

"What do you mean?"

"Lieutenant, it's no secret that you've grown pretty sweet on this girl. How do I know you weren't plotting something?"

"Plotting something? Plotting what?" Shields asked, exasperated.

"Maybe Manitoro's escape."

"Captain, have you gone crazy? I'm the one that captured him!" Shields exclaimed.

"Nevertheless, I can't take any chances. I'm placing you under house arrest. Go to your quarters. I will have guards posted. And you, young lady, return to the hospital. As soon as Chatoma is discharged, he will be forcibly removed to the San Carlos Indian Reservation. Since you are legally a white woman, you will not be allowed to go with him. Therefore, you'd better get your good-byes said now."

"Mark!" Sasha gasped. "Mark, no, don't let him do this!"

"Don't call to him for help. There's nothing he can do," Ross screamed. "Lieutenant, go to your quarters at once, or by God I'll have you put in irons."

Seething with anger, but knowing that in his state Ross might very well slap him in irons, Shields walked Sasha to the hospital and then retired to his quarters.

From the moment Farley Branson learned that Manitoro was a prisoner, he was worried. If Manitoro revealed Branson's involvement with his raids, it would ruin everything. Not only would Branson's dreams of a railroad empire be destroyed, but he might very well be hanged for treason or for complicity to commit murder. It did not matter what they got him on; either way he would be just as dead.

From a window in the front of the store, Branson watched Ross go to the guardhouse, and then a few minutes later he saw Lieutenant Shields and Sasha Quiet Stream walk away from there. Shields escorted the blond woman to the hospital and then went to his own quarters. After that, Ross staggered out of the guardhouse and returned to the party and his drinking. Branson breathed a little easier. Evidently Manitoro had said nothing yet; otherwise Ross would have had him arrested.

Branson stayed at the sutler's store until the party finally broke up. He sat in a chair and watched as the band members folded up their instruments and Wang came out of the back room to start picking up glasses. Captain Ross had passed out at a table in the back; other than the band, he was the only one remaining. The other partygoers had left, the civilians piling into carriages and wagons for the trip back into town.

"Bandmaster!" Branson called. "Would you please see to it that Captain Ross is returned to his quarters?"

"Yes, sir," the bandmaster, a white-haired, old master

sergeant answered. He ordered two of his bandsmen to handle the captain, and a few minutes later Wang retreated to
his four-by-eight cubicle. Then Branson had the place all to
himself.

He extinguished the lamps and then walked to the door
and stared across the dark compound toward the guardhouse.
At this late hour even the most confirmed reveler was in bed,
and an absolute stillness hung over the fort.

Branson stepped outside and then moved through the
darkness, staying in the shadows until he reached the guardhouse. He hid behind the corner until the guard came by on
his back-and-forth path. When the soldier turned, Branson
stepped out and clubbed him over the head with the handle
of his pistol. The guard collapsed in a heap.

Branson hurried over to the guardhouse door and opened
it. "Manitoro," he whispered. "Manitoro, it's me, Branson.
Hurry, I've knocked the guard out. Get out of here."

Manitoro got up and came toward the door, moving
slowly, wary of a trap.

"Hurry up," Branson hissed. "I didn't hit him all that
hard, he's not going to stay out all night."

"Why did you do this?" Manitoro asked. His blue eyes
coldly regarded Branson.

"Because we still have a little business to conduct,"
Branson said. "Meet me tomorrow at the ravine."

Manitoro nodded and slithered out of the guardhouse.
Without a backward glance he hurried through the night,
climbed the wall, looked around, and then jumped down to
the other side. Branson slipped back through the night to his
store, confident that Ross would believe that an Indian had
slipped in to free Manitoro.

Though Branson did not realize it, the guard had come
to, just as Branson and Manitoro were speaking. He over-
heard Branson say to Manitoro that they had a little business
to conduct and that they would meet the next day at the
ravine. He tried to get up to stop them, but even though he
was conscious, he was so groggy and so sick from the blow to
his head that he could not force himself to move. By the time
he was finally able to get up and turn in the alarm, it was too
late. Manitoro was over the wall, and Branson was back in
the store.

"The damnedest thing, Sergeant Major," the guard later told O'Braugh. "You'll never guess who let him out."

"Who was it?"

"The sutler, Mr. Branson."

The guard was one of O'Braugh's most trusted soldiers, and O'Braugh put his hand on the young man's shoulder. "Lad, don't say a word about this to anyone yet."

"Sergeant Major, the son of a bitch let Manitoro go! And besides that, he hit me over the head. I don't intend to let him get away with it!" the guard protested angrily.

"Aye, lad, I agree with you. And he won't get away with it. But if you'll keep quiet for a while, it may help us get Manitoro back. Trust me." O'Braugh looked at the soldier levelly and rested a large hand on his shoulder.

"All right, Sergeant Major. If you say so."

O'Braugh hurried through the darkness to Shields's quarters. He was surprised to see a guard on duty outside, but then he remembered that Shields had been placed on arrest-in-quarters.

"Halt! Who goes there?" the guard called.

"It's me, lad, Sergeant Major O'Braugh. Is the lieutenant still in his quarters?"

"Yes, Sergeant Major."

"Good lad, you're doin' a good job here."

"Sergeant Major, I don't feel right about this," the private said. "I think Lieutenant Shields is a good officer."

"Aye, that he is," O'Braugh said, nodding his head and smiling at the guard. "And I think this little misunderstandin's about to be cleared up. The captain sent me after the lieutenant. He wants to talk to him."

The guard hesitated for just a moment. O'Braugh knew that the soldier had been ordered to keep Lieutenant Shields in his quarters and that this was a definite change.

"What . . . what should I do, Sergeant Major?"

"Do? Do about what?" O'Braugh asked. He knew the trooper was questioning the procedure, and in truth the sergeant felt proud of him for being a good soldier.

"I'm supposed to stay right here until I'm properly relieved," the young man said.

O'Braugh smiled. "Sure an' you do that, trooper," he

said. "I've no authority to relieve you. You just stand guard like you been doin'."

"Yes, sir. Thank you, Sergeant Major." The soldier was thankful to have the situation spelled out for him. When O'Braugh and Shields left a moment later, the soldier snapped to attention sharply, and Shields saluted him.

"He's a good man," O'Braugh said softly as they slipped away into the shadows. "I hope you remember him."

"At my court-martial you mean?" Shields said jokingly.

"Don't even be thinkin' such a thing," O'Braugh protested. "Now we'll be gettin' the young lass, and then we'll go in search of Manitoro."

Because Shields was under arrest, he waited in the shadows of the hospital while O'Braugh awakened Amy Hartfield and asked her to fetch Sasha for him. A moment later Mrs. Hartfield came down the stairs with a puzzled expression on her face.

"She's not up there," Amy said.

"Are you sure she went up for the night?" O'Braugh asked.

"Yes, a couple of hours ago. Unless she's over in the hospital wing with her father. Would you like me to check there?"

"No, ma'am. I'll check," O'Braugh said. "Thank you, ma'am."

"I hope she's all right," Amy said, her voice clearly expressing her concern.

"I'm sure she is," O'Braugh replied soothingly.

In fact, O'Braugh was worried about her. She was not in her room, and he soon discovered that she was not with her father. Providing she was nowhere else on the post, that left only one possibility: Manitoro must have come back and taken her hostage.

Chapter Twelve

The Mazatzal Mountains rose like huge black slabs against the velvet texture of the sky. Overhead the stars spread their diamond glitter across the heavens, while far in the east a tiny bar of pearl-gray light gave the first hint of dawn.

The wind, which had moaned and whistled across the rocky crags and sharp precipices throughout the long night, had quieted now, and a stillness had come over the land. When the sun had risen and light streamed down on the desert floor, Shields reached for his hat. He shook it to make certain it was free of scorpions and, finding it safe, put it on his head. Unscrewing the cap of his canteen, he took a drink, then handed it to O'Braugh, who also took a drink and then put the cap back on. For both men the drink of water would serve as breakfast.

When the two men had left the fort in the middle of the night, they had decided the best way to find Manitoro would be to watch the road that Branson would have to take and then follow him when he kept his rendezvous. It was hard to sit and wait, especially since they believed Sasha was being held hostage, but they knew it was their best chance.

"I hope Branson keeps his appointment," O'Braugh said, handing the canteen back to Shields.

"He will," Shields replied. "It's all beginning to make sense to me now. Branson wants the land the Indians control. That's why he was trying to talk Chatoma into selling the grants to him. He figures to get it one way or the other—either by forcing Chatoma to sell to him, or by getting the

171

army to run all the Indians out, so he can pick it up for nothing. And unless I miss my guess, he's already bought out the ranchers and farmers who have been frightened away, too."

"What does he plan to do with the land once he has it?" O'Braugh asked.

"You remember the two businessmen who were here, Connell and Trapman?"

"The ones who were riding on Emily's stage the day she was attacked," O'Braugh said, nodding.

"Yes. Well, I checked on those gentlemen," Shields said. "They are in the railroad business."

"Why, that blackguard! He's tryin' to run Emily out of business!" O'Braugh exclaimed. "A railroad between Sedona and Prescott would kill the stage line. And he's been using Manitoro to do it for him."

"Yes. Though, from what little I learned of Manitoro last night, it's hard to believe he would make any kind of a deal with a white man, for any reason."

"Maybe the reason is in that wagon," O'Braugh said, pointing. Shields turned his head to follow O'Braugh's outstretched arm and saw a single wagon moving slowly across the rolling desert, far in the distance. "There goes Branson."

"All right," Shields said, standing up and brushing his hands together. "Let's follow him. With any luck, he'll lead us right to Manitoro."

There was a pounding in Ross's head that would not go away. He pulled the pillow over his head, but the pounding persisted. At last he realized that he was awake and that the pounding was not in his head but at the door. He opened his eyes and found that the bright, morning sunlight was painful to his eyes. He covered them with his hand and lay back on the pillow for a moment. His tongue was thick, and he tasted cotton in his mouth. He realized then that he was not in bed in his quarters; he was on the sofa in his office, still in his mess-dress uniform. For some reason, he had not gone home last night, though he could not remember why.

"Cap'n Ross, are you in there, sir?" a voice asked uneasily through the door.

Ross got up from the sofa and walked unsteadily to the door. When he opened it, he saw the first sergeant and the sergeant of the guard standing there. He waved them inside and then staggered over to the water bucket. Scooping out a dipper of water, he drank it thirstily, letting some of it run down his chin. He poured a second dipperful over his head and then rubbed his face and eyes. Finally he felt conscious enough to face the two noncoms.

"What?" he asked, turning around to look at the men. His tongue was still so thick he could barely talk.

"It's Manitoro, sir. He's gone."

"Gone? What do you mean gone? Gone from where?"

"Why, gone from the guardhouse, sir," the first sergeant said. "Don't you recall, he sneaked onto the post last night and tried to kill Lieutenant Shields. We caught him and put him in the guardhouse."

Ross could remember. It was fuzzy, almost as if it had been a dream, but he could remember. "Yes," he said slowly. "I remember. The girl, Sasha, she is Manitoro's sister?"

"Yes, sir. And that's the problem."

"What's the problem? Sergeant, you aren't making a lot of sense."

"The girl's gone too, sir. Sneaked out during the night."

"Damn!" Ross said, now coming wide awake. "She let him go?"

"We don't know whether she did or not. The guard was knocked out. He says he didn't see who done it."

"It's obvious, isn't it?" Ross said. "The girl let him out." He smiled. "Well, Sergeant, this makes things a lot easier, doesn't it? Now we know that Chatoma's people are right in the middle of things. Turn out the troops. I'm going to lead an expedition against Chatoma's camp."

"Sir, shouldn't we just send a few men out there to have a look around first?"

"No," Ross said firmly. "That would only alert them. We'll get into position, then wait until dark. The tactic that worked for us before will work again. We'll attack in the middle of the night."

Tying their horses to some brush, Shields and O'Braugh took extra ammunition from their saddlebags and slipped through the rocks down a hillside until they were nearly at Branson's wagon, which they had followed through the desert hills here to the craggy lower slopes of the Mazatzal Moun-

tains. Branson had stopped the wagon and left it behind as he
disappeared down a steep incline into a narrow, twisting
ravine. The wagon was obviously loaded, though a canvas
cover kept its contents hidden.

"Keep your eyes open for me," Shields said. "I'm going
down there to see what's under that tarpaulin."

"All right," O'Braugh said. He cocked his rifle and looked
toward the narrow crevice while Shields started toward the
wagon. The lieutenant moved down the hillside cautiously,
slipping behind the rocks in case Branson should rise up from
the deep ravine. It took him only a moment to get to the
wagon. When he did, he threw the canvas cover back and
caught his breath at what he saw. The wagon was loaded with
rifles and boxes of ammunition.

"I told you I'd make good on my word, Manitoro,"
Shields heard Branson say. "Come on up here and see what
I've got for you."

Branson and Manitoro, with a group of warriors behind
them, suddenly appeared at the head of the crevice, and
seeing Shields at the wagon, they let out a shout.

O'Braugh fired at Branson, but the bullet hit the stone
side of the crevice and ricocheted from side to side as it
worked its way through the deep, narrow passage. It hit no
one, but it did make Branson and the Indians duck back into
the crevice, giving Shields the time he needed to run back to
the rocks where O'Braugh had taken cover.

Because the passageway was so narrow, O'Braugh figured he had Branson and the Indians trapped inside. But
within moments he saw them crawling up the side. Surprised
by their boldness, O'Braugh turned around and looked up
the hill behind him. He was stunned by what he saw: scores
of Indians scrabbling down the side of the hill, working their
way among the rocks toward Shields and O'Braugh.

The two soldiers were facing overwhelming odds, with
attackers coming toward them from two sides, but the two
men were in a good defensive position, and both were deadly
shots.

"I'm thinkin' 'tis a shame we didn't take cover nearer
that wagon, lad," O'Braugh said when Shields told him what
was under the tarpaulin. "I'd be given' my eye teeth for that
ammunition right now."

Manitoro's warriors paid dearly during the first minutes

of the gunfight that followed. When one of the Indians felt a urge of bravery and charged forward toward the two soldiers, either Shields or O'Braugh was able to take accurate aim and hit the attacker. Finally Manitoro stopped his warriors from squandering their lives so foolishly. Instead he spread them out among the rocks and began advancing them a little at a time, each man moving from rock to rock as the noose around O'Braugh and Shields slowly tightened.

"Lad," O'Braugh said, just after one of his shots had sent an approaching Indian scurrying back behind a rock. "How are you on ammunition?"

"I think I have three rounds remaining in the magazine," Shields said. "That's all. How about you?"

"I just used my last one," O'Braugh said.

Shields operated the lever on his rifle and jacked out one of his shells. He handed the shell to O'Braugh, who slipped it into his own rifle and then jacked it into the chamber.

"Don't fire again until their final charge," Shields said.

"Aye. I'm only regrettin' that Branson is safe behind the rocks. I'd gladly use my last bullet on his black heart."

The two men waited, and though the Indians continued to fire sporadically, they did not return the fire.

"Lieutenant!" Manitoro called. "You are out of bullets, aren't you?"

"Why don't you come down here and find out?" Shields replied.

"I will," Manitoro replied. "I will."

"Good. I'm waiting for you."

One of the Indians, perhaps emboldened by the thought that the two soldiers were out of ammunition, stood up and started running toward them. Yelling loudly, he brandished his war club, intending to finish them off by hand, thus earning the respect and admiration of the others. Shields took slow, deliberate aim and then squeezed the trigger. The foolhardy brave went down with a hole in his forehead.

"Well," Shields said quietly. "We've one shot each, now."

"And I'll not spend it till I can send one more heathen to hell," O'Braugh promised.

There was a long period of silence. Then the Indians started firing again, working closer to the two cavalrymen. O'Braugh raised up to see where they were moving, and a bullet hit a rock so close to him that chips flew into his face, cutting his cheek. He put his finger to his cheek and then wiped it away and looked at the blood.

"Well, lad," he said. "Since I'm thinkin' we'll soon be in Fiddlers' Green, would you be for joinin' your father an' me for drinks tonight?"

"Kevin O'Braugh, I can think of no better company to while away eternity with," Shields said with a smile.

Suddenly the sound of gunfire doubled in intensity, and the two men realized with surprise that the shooting was coming from a new quarter.

"The saints be praised," O'Braugh said. "The army's come to our rescue!"

"No!" Shields said, pointing and shaking his head. "Look! It isn't the army, it's Sasha!"

O'Braugh peered in the direction Shields had indicated, and then he exclaimed, "The girl wasn't snatched! She left to get her own people!"

The Indians who had been steadily advancing on Shields and O'Braugh's position turned and began running. Some of them tried to return the fire, but the battle was brief and furious. Within moments, dozens of them lay dead.

Manitoro managed to make it back into the crevice, and once there, protected from the fire of Sasha's braves, he started into the deep ravine. He knew a back way out.

"Manitoro!" Branson suddenly shouted. Manitoro looked over to see the civilian standing behind a rock. Branson had found shelter there when the fighting had started with Shields and O'Braugh. Now he and Manitoro were alone, and he was pointing a rifle toward the renegade.

"What are you doing?" Manitoro asked.

Branson smiled. "I'm afraid I can't let you live," he said. "If I kill you now, I can claim that I used the weapons as bait. I'll say I suckered you into a trap, and Captain Ross will back me up."

"So," Manitoro said. "You think you can kill me? I am Manitoro! I cannot be killed by a store clerk."

"You know what amazes me? That you, a white man, can really believe that," Branson said. He raised the rifle to his shoulder.

Manitoro carried his own rifle, but it was in his left hand, hanging down by his side, and he knew he would not have time to raise it and fire. But his knife was in a scabbard on his right thigh. In an instant he had it in his hand and with a flip of his wrist sent it flying toward Branson—in the same instant that Branson fired.

As Shields and Sasha were embracing, one of her warriors said something to them in the Apache tongue.

"Mark, he said Branson is still alive," Sasha said.

"Take me to him," Shields told the Indian, and he and Sasha followed through the long, narrow crevice until they came to the open part of the ravine. There, it was easy to see what had happened. Manitoro was lying on his back, his eyes open and clouded. A small, black hole was in his chest, just over his heart. No more than thirty feet away from him Branson was leaning against a rock. The front of his shirt was covered with blood, and the handle of a knife was sticking out from his chest.

"I . . . I can't seem to pull it out," Branson gasped.

"I'll do it," Shields offered.

"No," Branson said. "Leave it. I'm dying anyway."

"You have anything you want to say? Any last words?" Shields asked.

"You mean something noble? Something you can carve on my tombstone?" Branson asked. He tried to laugh, but the laugh turned into a racking, painful cough.

"No. I mean why you did all this."

"That should be easy enough to understand," Branson said, his voice a rasping whisper. "I wanted to build a railroad."

"And Ross? Is he a part of it?"

"Ross? Can you believe it? He was a pretty good soldier in his day. Now he's nothing but a rumpot." He paused to catch his breath. "No, he had nothing to do with it. He was too dumb—or too drunk—to know what was going on. I had him so much in debt to me that I could hang him out to turn slowly in the wind, and there was nothing he could do about it." He started laughing again, and again the laugh erupted into a racking cough. Then a rattling, wheezing sound came from his throat, and finally he drew his last breath.

"Branson? Branson?"

"He's dead, lad."

Shields looked up to see O'Braugh standing over him.

"Did you hear what he said about Ross? How Ross was not involved in his scheme?"

"Aye, I heard," O'Braugh said. " 'Tis good to see the cap'n didn't sink that far."

Shields saw Sasha looking down at her brother's body, and he walked over to stand beside her. He put his arm around her, and she nestled into the comfort of his arm.

"He pushed me under the wagon," Sasha said quietly, her eyes filmed with tears.

"What?" Shields looked at her, puzzled.

"I remember now. When we were attacked, the wagon turned over, and Jimmy pushed me under so I could hide. He was a good boy then. I know I should not feel sad now. But I do."

Shields thought of the young boy who, though he was beaten every day, would not let the Indian boys see him cry. "You can feel sad for Jimmy," Shields said. "He deserved someone to feel sad for him. It's Manitoro that the world is better off without."

They made a curious sight as they came through the gates of the fort later that day. Mark Shields and Sasha Quiet Stream rode side by side in front of Branson's wagon, which was driven by Kevin O'Braugh. Inside the wagon, in addition to the rifles and ammunition Branson had taken to the Indians, were the bodies of Branson and Manitoro. Tied to the rear of the wagon was O'Braugh's horse.

As soon as they were inside the gate, the band broke into a rousing march, and Shields was surprised to see the entire garrison turned out in parade formation. Of course, the men at the fort knew what had happened, because Sasha had sent a fast rider back to take them the news. Still, the parade was unexpected.

"Sergeant Major!" Shields called, turning in the saddle. "Leave the wagon and get mounted."

"Yes, sir," O'Braugh said. A moment later, mounted, O'Braugh pulled his horse up alongside Shields's. Sasha started to ride away from them, but Shields reached out to stop her.

"No," he said, shaking his head and smiling. "This is as much your honor as it is ours. And I want you beside me, now and forever."

Beaming brightly at his words, Sasha rode beside him as Shields led them past the troops. Then Shields, O'Braugh, and Sasha rode to the head of the formation. Standing under the flagpole to receive his salute was Major James Hartfield.

"Sir, Second Lieutenant Shields and Sergeant Major O'Braugh reporting," he said, rendering a hand salute.

"At ease, Lieutenant," Major Hartfield said. "Adjutant, read the orders."

"Yes, sir," the adjutant said. He cleared his throat and began to read. "Attention to orders. Captain Alan Ross, U.S. Cavalry, is hereby relieved of command and all duties and functions pertaining to command of Fort Verde, Arizona Territory. Second Lieutenant Mark Shields, U.S. Cavalry, is hereby appointed to the permanent rank of first lieutenant and breveted a major for the purpose of assuming command of Fort Verde, Arizona Territory. For the Commander, E. E. Thompson, First Lieutenant, Adjutant."

"Major Shields, the command is yours, sir," Hartfield said, saluting Shields and grinning broadly.

Shields, overwhelmed by what was going on, looked over at O'Braugh. "What do I do?" he whispered.

"Well, sir, you can start by gettin' the troops out of the noonday sun," O'Braugh said, and he began to laugh.

"Good idea," Shields said, chuckling. He dismissed the garrison, and they promptly sent up three rousing cheers for their new commander. When the shouting had died down, Shields turned to Hartfield. "Where's Ross?"

"Amy and Emily have prepared lunch for us," Hartfield said, brushing aside his question with a wave of his hand. "The three of you come along, and I'll explain everything."

"Emily's here?" O'Braugh asked. It was his turn to be surprised.

Hartfield laughed. "Now, did you think she'd be in Prescott while you were gone, Sergeant Major?"

When they entered the parlor of the Hartfields' house, Shields saw that not only were Emily and Amy there, but so was Chatoma. The three smiling friends were seated in a cluster of chairs at the far end of the room. Shields had never seen Chatoma looking so well. The old chief's eyes were sparkling brightly, his face was no longer pale, and the clothes he wore could only be described as ceremonial.

"Father!" Sasha said, hurrying over to his chair to embrace him.

"He's fit as a fiddle," Major Hartfield said as he stood in the doorway, smiling at the group.

"Good," Shields said, and he turned to the chief with a wide smile. "Are you well enough to put together an Indian police force? Some of Manitoro's warriors escaped. I think we need to round them up."

Chatoma beamed delightedly. "I have long asked the army to let us have a police force of our own," he said. "But the army has always said we could not do this."

"If I understand these orders, I'm the army now," Shields said. "That is right, isn't it?" he asked Hartfield.

"Yes, sir, that is quite correct," Hartfield said, and a little smile played at his lips.

"Chatoma, you have your police force," Shields said.

"Thank you," Chatoma said. "This will mean the end of war between our people for all time."

"Now," Shields said, turning to Hartfield. "You were going to tell me about Ross."

Major Hartfield drew a deep breath and then explained that, as the medical officer, he had no command responsibility, but he could declare a person unfit for duty. As a result of Captain Ross's irrational behavior and excessive drinking lately, the doctor had wired Washington, declaring the captain no longer fit for command by virtue of alcoholism.

"He planned to take the troop out to Chatoma's village," Hartfield went on. "He was going to attack them tonight. Instead, he had another bout with the bottle, and we found him passed out in his office. I had him moved to the hospital. His quarters are now your quarters."

Shields looked at Sasha. "Our quarters," he said softly. He looked over at Chatoma. "I've asked her to marry me—provided I don't have to come up with a herd of horses to get your blessing," he teased.

"Maybe only four—" Chatoma began, but Sasha interrupted him.

"Father!" she cried indignantly.

"Three."

"Father," she said again.

"Daughter, it dishonors you if your man will not pay something of great value for you," Chatoma complained.

"Wait," Shields said. "I do have something. I must go to

my quarters, but I'll be right back." He turned and rushed from the parlor.

Sasha and the others waited patiently until Shields returned a few moments later, carrying something large and square, wrapped in paper. When he unwrapped it, everyone in the room gasped in amazement. It was a painting—not a drawing, but a full-color oil painting. In it a young warrior sat on a horse on the edge of a butte, peering intently out over the Arizona desert. The warrior was young, powerful, and handsome. And as they looked more closely they saw that, despite the absence of wrinkles and the blackness of the hair, it was Chatoma.

Chatoma reached out to touch the painting. Then he touched his own face. His eyes glistened brightly, and if Shields had wanted to embarrass him, he could have pointed out that the glistening came from a film of tears.

"Look," Chatoma said in an awestruck voice. "I will be forever young."

"I give you this as a present for your daughter," Shields said.

"Yes," Chatoma said, nodding his head enthusiastically. "Yes."

"That's quite a talent for a military man," Hartfield observed.

"Thanks," Shields said. He looked at Sasha and smiled. "But I think I should tell you now. I don't intend to be a military man forever."

"I didn't think you would be," Hartfield said.

"Sergeant Major, I hope you aren't disappointed," Shields went on. "But I'm only going to hold this position until the new commander arrives. Then I'm going to resign and do what I really want to do. Sasha and I are going to tour the West, chronicling the life of whites and Indians on the frontier. I already have a letter of agreement with *Harper's Weekly*. They'll pay quite handsomely for the pictures."

"Lad, you've more than fulfilled anything you might have felt you owed to your father's name," O'Braugh said. "Sure an' I'd be disappointed if you didn't follow your dream. And now, if I might be so bold, I'd like to ask the commander for permission to be takin' a wife of my own."

Emily gasped aloud, and everyone looked over at her.

Sasha, smiling warmly, moved to her side and gave her a hug.

"Are you sure about this, Sergeant Major?" Shields teased. "A confirmed bachelor asking for permission to marry?"

"Aye, lad," O'Braugh replied. "After all, I once told you I'd soak my trousers in coal oil an' march to hell to see you kick the devil himself in the behind. I believe in following my commander . . . into battle or into matrimony." Suddenly he realized that he had left out one little detail, and he turned to Emily. "That is, if the woman I've in mind will be havin' me."

"If it's me, you old coot," Emily said laughing, "I'll be havin' you an' proud of it. If it's not me but someone else you're after, then you needn't be worryin' about soakin' your trousers in coal oil and marchin' off to hell, for I'll take care of that little task for you myself."

They all shared a good laugh, and then Amy called the women over to make plans for a double wedding at the post chapel. Outside they could hear the notes of the bugler as he played "Boots and Saddles," calling the men to duty at Fort Verde.

Coming in Spring 1989
WAGONS WEST
VOLUME XXIII
OKLAHOMA!
by Dana Fuller Ross

The great American epic continues in volume twenty-three of the landmark series that has made publishing history with more than 25,000,000 copies in print.

Intrepid Toby Holt, frontiersman and business-man extraordinaire, is called upon to bring peace to an Oklahoma town torn apart by violence and greed . . .

Meanwhile, the other daring men and passion-ate women whom millions of readers have come to love will pursue their destinies from the expanse of the West to the distant corners of the world—as the American pioneer spirit takes them on far-flung adventures that will stir the heart and quicken the imagination.

Don't miss the next volume in this bestselling historical series. Read OKLAHOMA!—wherever Bantam Books are sold.

★ WAGONS WEST ★

A series of unforgettable books that trace the lives of a dauntless band of pioneering men, women, and children as they brave the hazards of an untamed land in their trek across America. This legendary caravan of people forge a new link in the wilderness. They are Americans from the North and the South, alongside immigrants, Blacks, and Indians, who wage fierce daily battles for survival on this uncompromising journey—each to their private destinies as they fulfill their greatest dreams.

☐	26822	INDEPENDENCE! #1	$4.50
☐	26162	NEBRASKA! #2	$4.50
☐	26242	WYOMING! #3	$4.50
☐	26072	OREGON! #4	$4.50
☐	26070	TEXAS! #5	$4.50
☐	26377	CALIFORNIA! #6	$4.50
☐	26546	COLORADO! #7	$4.50
☐	26069	NEVADA! #8	$4.50
☐	26163	WASHINGTON! #9	$4.50
☐	26073	MONTANA! #10	$4.50
☐	26184	DAKOTA! #11	$4.50
☐	26521	UTAH! #12	$4.50
☐	26071	IDAHO! #13	$4.50
☐	26367	MISSOURI! #14	$4.50
☐	27141	MISSISSIPPI! #15	$4.50
☐	25247	LOUISIANA! #16	$4.50
☐	25622	TENNESSEE! #17	$4.50
☐	26022	ILLINOIS! #18	$4.50
☐	26533	WISCONSIN! #19	$4.50
☐	26849	KENTUCKY! #20	$4.50
☐	27065	ARIZONA! #21	$4.50

Prices and availability subject to change without notice.

Bantam Books, Dept. LE, 414 East Golf Road, Des Plaines, IL 60016

Please send me the books I have checked above. I am enclosing $_____ (please add $2.00 to cover postage and handling). Send check or money order—no cash or C.O.D.s please.

Mr/Ms _____

Address _____

City/State _____ Zip _____

LE—11/88

Please allow four to six weeks for delivery. This offer expires 5/89.

Special Offer
Buy a Bantam Book
for only 50¢.

Now you can have Bantam's catalog filled with hundreds of titles plus take advantage of our unique and exciting bonus book offer. A special offer which gives you the opportunity to purchase a Bantam book for only 50¢. Here's how!

By ordering any five books at the regular price per order, you can also choose any other single book listed (up to a $5.95 value) for just 50¢. Some restrictions do apply, but for further details why not send for Bantam's catalog of titles today!

Just send us your name and address and we will send you a catalog!

BANTAM BOOKS, INC.
P.O. Box 1006, South Holland, Ill. 60473

Mr./Mrs./Ms. _____
(please print)

Address _____

City _____ State _____ Zip _____

FC(A)—10/87

Please allow four to six weeks for delivery.